THE
FRIENDSHIP
DOLL

THE
FRIENDSHIP
DOLL

KIRBY LARSON

DELACORTE PRESS

Text copyright © 2011 by Kirby Larson
Jacket art copyright © 2011 by Beth White

All rights reserved. Published in the United States by Delacorte Press, an imprint of Random House Children's Books, a division of Random House, Inc., New York.

Delacorte Press is a registered trademark and the colophon is a trademark of Random House, Inc.

Visit us on the Web! www.randomhouse.com/kids
Educators and librarians, for a variety of teaching tools,
visit us at www.randomhouse.com/teachers.

Library of Congress Cataloging-in-Publication Data
Larson, Kirby.
    The friendship doll / Kirby Larson. — 1st ed.
        p. cm.
    Summary: Throughout the twentieth century, Miss Kanagawa, one of fifty-eight dolls made to serve as ambassadors from Japan to the United States, travels the country learning to love while changing the lives of those who need her.
    ISBN 978-0-385-73745-6 (hc : alk. paper) — ISBN 978-0-375-89951-5 (ebook) — ISBN 978-0-385-90667-8 (glb : alk. paper) [1. Dolls—Fiction. 2. Ambassadors—Fiction. 3. Conduct of life—Fiction. 4. United States—History—20th century—Fiction.] I. Title.
PZ7.L32394Fr 2011   [Fic]—dc22   2010020615

The text of this book is set in 12¼-point Goudy.
Book design by Vikki Sheatsley
Printed in the United States of America
10 9 8 7 6 5 4 3 2 1
First Edition

Random House Children's Books supports the First Amendment and celebrates the right to read.

For Tyler,
who has his own stories to tell

Beginnings

When the Japanese give a doll in friendship, it is bestowed with great meaning and honor. . . . Even adults speak about dolls as though they were almost human. A doll is not simply stored in a box. She sleeps waiting for a child to wake her.

—JAMIE TOBIAS NEELY
The Spokesman-Review (Spokane, Washington)
MARCH 3, 1993

Kanagawa Prefecture, Japan

Master Doll-Maker Tatsuhiko

The old doll-maker Tatsuhiko poured boiling water into the teapot with trembling hands and inhaled deeply. It was the last of his tea. He portioned out his breakfast rice and took a seat on a tatami mat. One of the blessings of growing old was that it did not take much to make his stomach content. And this morning his heart was so full that food seemed trivial.

Tatsuhiko studied the doll he had completed the night before, smoothing an almost invisible tangle in her black hair. Miss Kanagawa. She would be the last doll he would ever make. *Could* ever make. His hands shook so these days, and his eyes were full of clouds. It was difficult to think his doll-making days were ended, but, like bitter tea, this fact was best swallowed down quickly.

Though he wasn't like Kurita—a man whose endless boasts clanged like the chappa cymbal—he *was* proud of his efforts. His wife would be, too, were she still living. Miss Kanagawa was a doll like none other. The size of a five-year-old girl, she was even more exquisite than the doll he'd made for the infant Empress. Two hands like graceful lilies rested at her sides. Her eyes, so clear and proud, gazed into his own. Her delicate cherry lips parted slightly, as if she were on the verge of speaking to him. He was almost disappointed not to hear her speak, but he knew she'd been created for the children in the Land of the Stars, and not for him.

He had dressed her in their daughter's best kimono, in its rich print of blue chrysanthemums against orange silk. This was the very one his wife had stitched for the child's fifth birthday. Her last birthday. Tatsuhiko's heart had shriveled like a dried plum the day the sickness took their sweet daughter away.

"You look lovely, little sister." The old doll-maker dabbed at his eyes. The steamy tea must be making them water. "I know you will serve your new role well, and will carry the message of friendship honorably. But my wish is that you will find a doll's true purpose: to be awakened by the heart of a child." He fussed with the obi until it was tied just so and then gently wrapped the doll in a blanket.

Yoshitoku Doll Company was a mile across town, but the walk there was too short, even for his old legs. Too soon, Tatsuhiko was unwrapping Miss Kanagawa from the

4

blanket, handing her over to the owner of the company. "Safe travels, little sister," he said, patting her long black hair. His troublesome eyes began to water again.

"Will you not enjoy some tea before you go?" The doll company owner was concerned for this frail man whose head bobbed like a koi at feeding time.

But Tatsuhiko declined. "My wife waits for me," he said. And without another glance at his creation, his masterpiece, he turned and shuffled away.

Arrival in America

DOLLS TO BEAR GOOD-WILL
Japanese Children Are Sending Them to Show Friendship for Us

TOKIO, NOV. 5, 1927 (AP) — Fifty-eight Japanese dolls, messengers of friendship from the children of Japan to the children of the United States, received their formal farewell yesterday from 1,500 Japanese schoolgirls in a ceremony preceding the sailing of the dolls for San Francisco aboard the steamship *Tenyo Maru,* which will leave Japan on Thursday.

The children read addresses expressing hopes that the doll gifts to the American schoolchildren, presented in appreciation for more than 10,000 dolls, which American children gave for the doll festival of Japanese girls, will carry the assurances of Japanese friendship for the United States.

The Japanese and American anthems were sung at the ceremony and Ambassador MacVeigh and Viscount Shibusawa made speeches.

✳

MISS KANAGAWA

This leg of our journey, from Washington, D.C., to New York City, we are riding as befits our rank—finally!—sitting in seats, rather than closed up in our trunks, in the luggage compartment, hidden away from the exciting sights and sounds of this country called America. Elder Sister, Miss Japan, is on my right, unusually quiet. It has been some time since she has offered advice about proper behavior for a Doll Ambassador. Not that I need her lectures, but others of our fifty-six sisters certainly do. Miss Tokushima, for example. Weeping and wailing as we departed Japan. Shameful.

It is no small sacrifice that I will not see my homeland again. But I will shed no tears, choosing instead to live up to the honorable task bestowed upon me: strengthening the bonds of friendship between two proud countries. Such a mission requires true samurai spirit. Sadly, some of my sisters are lacking in such spirit.

I will let you judge *my* fitness by stating certain facts. When the *Tenyo Maru* sailed out of Tokyo, I was the first of my doll sisters to turn a brave face west, to accept my new life. I rode courageously through the city on the back of a motorcycle when we arrived in San Francisco. And I'm sure you can guess which of us greeted the American president's wife, yesterday in Washington, D.C., with dry palms and calm confidence.

Make no mistake! This job has not been all peach blossoms and tea cakes. I've endured my share of dolts who point and stare and think me from China. And, though offended to the core, I was outwardly serene when that one young girl asked if I could say "Mama" or wet. Perish the thought!

None have heard me grumble—not once!—about all those grimy hands patting my kimono, that parting gift from Master Doll-Maker Tatsuhiko. He said he hoped that I would find my true purpose. Poor man—his longing to be with his daughter and wife had made a tangle of his thoughts. I *know* what my true purpose is. It is to be an ambassador beyond compare. And this kimono—lovelier than those of any of my sisters—is a fitting gown for one such as I.

Yes, Master Tatsuhiko would be proud of me. Through a multitude of indignities, I have worn a steadfast smile, holding my lily hands out to all in goodwill.

Miss Japan's thoughts stir. *It is when we have had our hearts awakened by a child that we can truly call ourselves ambassadors of friendship.*

My heart has been open to all, I protest.

I hear the smug sigh of a know-too-much.

We none of us have hearts. Yet. Miss Japan settles onto the seat, her eyes closing with a soft click.

I know from the fuzzy silence that she is asleep. There will be no more lectures—for a time.

All the same, her words nettle like a patch of thorns. Is it not enough that I have thus far played my role beyond reproach? Now, apparently, I must be like the plum tree that sacrifices precious leaves and fruit to a worm. Only *my* worm will be a child.

I shudder and then push my thoughts in more pleasant directions.

Miss Japan may think of herself as a doll, dependent on a child's love for fulfillment. My other sisters may feel this way, too. That is their affair. But I am above all an ambassador, a dignitary. I simply happen to be a doll.

A doll with as much use for a child as a dog has for a flea.

❋

Bunny Harnden

Applesauce!

Bunny stood on the top step at Mrs. Newcomb's Academy for Young Girls, careful to avoid getting slush on her new white kid boots, peering around the statue of the school's namesake to watch for Carson. Most of the other fifth-levels were in a knot on the far side of the landing. It'd been that way since Bunny started at Mrs. Newcomb's in the fall, but today she didn't give a fig about those other girls. Just wait until they saw her name and picture in the paper. That would show them.

Father's new Minerva Town Car glided up to the curb. Carson stepped out and came around to open the door. With a posture that would've made their beleaguered charm teacher proud, Bunny swept down the fifteen marble steps—head high, shoulders back—placing her feet daintily to keep her boots dry. She paused in profile before slipping into the backseat. As Carson closed the door, Bunny stole a quick peek out the window, catching Belle Roosevelt sticking her tongue out at her. Bunny didn't even bother to stick her tongue out in return. Absolutely nothing was going to spoil her day. Nothing! Not even the assignment to parse out twenty-five sentences for English class by tomorrow.

She skipped through the door at home when Nanny opened it.

"And who did you sit with at lunch today?" Nanny asked. It was her way of finding out if Bunny had made any new friends yet.

"I studied for my Latin exam at lunch," Bunny answered. She wiggled out of her fox-trimmed wool wrapper and handed it to the old lady. "Is Mother home?"

Nanny smoothed the fur on the wrapper's collar. "Your mother and sister are engaged. Do you mind taking your tea in your room?"

"Oh." Bunny could see Mother and Winnifred with their heads together over something in the morning room, tea things scattered about. The two of them were always up to something together and were even busier lately, with that wretched coming-out party for Win. But not even taking tea alone was going to dampen Bunny's spirits. "No, I don't mind," she answered in her bravest voice. Bunny's boot heels click-clicked emphatically across the entry floor, but neither Mother nor Win even looked up. With a deep sigh, Bunny climbed the main staircase, one wide tread at a time.

"Slip those boots off and put them by the fire to dry," Nanny called after her. "Or you'll catch your death."

Bunny had changed out of her school uniform and was starting her homework when Nanny brought in the tea things. According to Mother, Bunny wasn't old enough for real tea. She generally got warm milk with honey and cinnamon.

"I have an errand for your mother, otherwise I'd sit and keep you company." Nanny picked up the doll Mother had ordered from France last year and placed it at the small table in Bunny's room. "You can have tea with your dolly. Won't that be lovely?"

She scurried out of the room without waiting for an answer, off again on one of the countless missions Mother—or rather, Win—required these days.

"Poor Nanny," Bunny said, reaching for a sliver of pound cake. "I'm eleven years old and she thinks I still play with dolls." She popped the cake into her mouth and brushed the crumbs from her hands. With a gulp that would've horrified Mother, Bunny downed the warm milk and then cleared the tea tray from the table. She wiped her hands on her skirt before lifting the Box from its hiding place under her bed. "Crayola Gold Medal School Crayons." Even the label was thrilling! There were eight in all: black, brown, blue, green, orange, red, violet, and yellow. Thicker than a pencil, they fit perfectly in her hand. And the waxiness made them so much more satisfying than colored pencils. Leave it to Grandfather to send her such a perfect gift.

She reached for the drawing, rolled into a neat scroll under the bed. It was safe here from prying eyes. She didn't want anyone to see it until it was completely finished. She'd worked on it for weeks, starting the very night that Mr. Reyburn, president of Lord & Taylor, one of the oldest and best shops on Fifth Avenue, had telephoned to ask Father if Bunny might like to try out to give a speech. The occasion would be a welcome ceremony for some Friendship Ambassador Dolls sent from Japan. Bunny had said yes straightaway. Even though she always got high marks in elocution, she could scarcely sleep for two nights afterward for the excitement of it.

She wasn't worried about being selected to speak. No. What had her on cloud nine was the notion of finally, finally, being able to command attention at the dinner table, contributing to conversation that had been dominated as of late by guest lists and cucumber sandwiches. Winnifred would have to listen to Bunny, for once. Mother, too.

Bunny smoothed out her drawing, the pleasure at what she'd created so far wrapping around her like a cozy cashmere shawl. There she was, center stage at the welcome ceremony, delivering her speech, a vision in a soft green dress. She had accomplished this effect by holding the Crayola lightly in her hand, gently stroking at the paper. She'd gotten the idea while watching Mother put on some face powder one morning.

In the drawing, the dolls—she knew there were to be five in all—were arrayed behind her. She reached for the black Crayola to color in their hair. Their costumes couldn't be colored in until after she saw them tomorrow. Next she would work on Father, but she had yet to decide whether to use violet or red on the flower in his lapel. There had been no room in the drawing for Winnifred. Too bad.

All the while she colored, Bunny recited her speech aloud. It was perfect, if she did say so herself. A thought snuck up on her. What if the *Times* wanted to include it in the article about the ceremony? After dinner, she'd write out a copy in her best penmanship. Just in case.

Happily absorbed in her art project, Bunny didn't realize she'd been called to supper until Nanny appeared in the doorway, all in a dither.

"Little miss, wash up quick and come." Nanny clapped her hands. "You're late." Lateness was a thing not tolerated in the Harnden household.

In a flash, Bunny rolled up her drawing and slid it and the box of Crayolas back into their hidey-hole.

Bunny did a quick washup, as instructed, lacing on her now-dry boots. She fairly floated down the stairs to the dining room, certain she couldn't eat a bite. She was far too excited about tomorrow's welcome ceremony. Maybe she could even wear Mother's pearls. After all, Mother was letting Win borrow them for the tea.

"Ah, there you are, Bunny." Mother sat, hands folded in her lap.

15

Bunny paused in the doorway. Long enough to etch in her mind this last evening of being a person of no consequence. Then she swept across the parquet floor to her place at the family table.

She unfolded her napkin, placed it on her lap, and reached for her fork.

"It's lovely news, isn't it, dear?" Mother said to Father.

Bunny sat up straighter. Children were to be seen, not heard. That was Mother's rule. But she could hardly contain herself. Mother's news would be lovely indeed. Even though she detested them, Bunny forked up a bite of brussels sprouts.

"Oh, yes." Father fussed with his roast beef, clearly fighting the urge to pick up the newspaper at his elbow. He so loved to read the *Times* at the dinner table. "What news would that be?" he asked, now focusing on Mother.

"Why, that call from Mr. Reyburn. About the welcome ceremony for those dolls tomorrow."

Bunny nearly leaped out of her skin. She was dying to hear the words from Mother's mouth. The words that would make her family pay attention to her.

Father searched around the table for the horseradish sauce. Finding it, he again looked at Mother. "I don't recall speaking to Mr. Reyburn today," he said.

Mother laughed lightly. "You didn't speak to him, darling. You were out. I left a message on your desk."

Bunny thought she would faint from the anticipation. She ate another bite of brussels sprouts without even noticing.

"I overlooked it somehow." His slice of roast beef well sauced with horseradish, Father ate a bite, then gestured with his empty fork for Mother to continue.

"Well," said Mother, "he said it was a difficult decision about the speaker, but he has decided." She fairly beamed.

Bunny wiggled like a pup.

"He's selected Belle Wyatt Roosevelt to speak."

Bunny's fork dropped with a huge clatter on her dinner plate. She couldn't believe her ears.

"My good Spode!" Mother exclaimed. "Be careful, dear."

"It's not fair." Bunny crumpled up her linen napkin and tossed it on the table. This couldn't be happening. She'd done her best. She'd been the best! "The only reason they picked Belle is because she's Mr. Teddy Roosevelt's granddaughter. It should've been me."

"Speaking of the Roosevelts," Winnifred interrupted, "I nearly forgot to put Penelope on the guest list."

"Must you always be on about that odious list?" Bunny's boot heels hit the chair rung with a satisfying clunk. If she heard one more word about her sister's coming-out tea, she might just run away.

"Bunny"—Mother's tone had a warning in it, one Bunny had heard many times before—"Belle is a lovely girl. Impeccable manners." Manners were everything in Mother's book. She could even give that Mrs. Emily Post a tip or two on etiquette.

Bunny turned to the other end of the table. "Father,

17

you said Mr. Reyburn told you I gave the prettiest speech of all the girls. Belle forgot most of hers!"

"No sour grapes, Bun." Father disappeared behind the *New York Times*. Bunny's eyes were drawn to the newspaper's motto: "All the News That's Fit to Print." Applesauce! *She* was supposed to have been in tomorrow's edition of that very paper, in an article that would have described how she had accepted one of the Japanese Friendship Dolls on behalf of all of the people of New York in a gracious and tasteful manner. With a photograph, too. And they would've printed her name all out in that civilized way the *Times* did: Miss Genevieve Harnden.

She'd worked so hard on her speech—"Mr. Charles Lindbergh inspires us to be bold, Gertrude Ederle inspires us to pursue our dreams, but these Doll Ambassadors from Japan inspire us to offer friendship wherever we go"—and she hadn't stumbled once in delivering it. Belle Wyatt Roosevelt not only stammered throughout the tryout, her speech had been as dull as a dishrag. And she was mean, besides. What about the way she'd tormented Mary Louise Miller after Mary Louise had botched that geography exam?

Bunny pushed her chair in, banging it against the dining table. "If I can't give my speech, I'm not going."

"You're part of the Welcome Committee." Mother pressed her napkin to her lips. "Of course you'll go."

"I won't. I won't!" Bunny stamped her foot. "It's not fair."

"That's enough, Genevieve." Father lowered his paper. "To your room."

"Don't you see, Mother?" Winnifred whined as Bunny clomped out of the dining room. "She'll absolutely ruin my tea if she comes."

It was no great punishment to leave the table. Bunny was sick to death of Winnifred's endless prattle about what kinds of flowers would be best on the tables—"Gardenias are so overdone, don't you think, Mumsy?"—and what she would wear. "Everyone's in transparent velvet this year," Winnifred had insisted. She'd demanded a gown in robin's-egg blue, to set off her eyes. If Win didn't want gardenias because everyone else had them, why wear a gown like all the other girls were wearing? It was all very confusing to Bunny.

Bunny's plan was to be so disagreeable for the next five years that there would be no fear at all of Mother giving a coming-out party for *her*. Look what was happening with Win's—transforming her from a perfectly intelligent and amusing sister into a pudding head. A pudding head in transparent blue velvet.

Bunny had had such high hopes that her speech in honor of those Doll Ambassadors would catapult her into Life, with a capital *L*. Father would have been so proud. And Mother might have seen how grown-up Bunny was becoming—ready for real tea and so much more. Those stuck-ups in her class who thought they were too ritzy for words would have invited Bunny to play sleeping lion at recess or sit with them at lunchtime. It was supposed to have been Bunny's big day. And now to learn that it would be Belle Roosevelt—the snake who had sunk so low as to launch into a fake coughing fit when Bunny was speaking at the tryout—with her photograph and name in the paper . . . well, it was too much to bear.

Stomping up each step of the grand staircase did nothing to stomp out her bitterness. Feeling alone and defeated, she snuck into Nanny's narrow room, off Bunny's own bedroom, and pilfered the last two coconut creams from Nanny's box of birthday chocolates. Nanny's memory was as flimsy as Win's new gown. She'd no doubt think that she herself had eaten them. Bunny gobbled both chocolates greedily, chomping hard, as if taking a good-sized bite out of that dreadful Belle Roosevelt's arm.

Bunny licked her fingers and swallowed. The sugar in her mouth did nothing to sweeten her mood. Once the last bit of chocolate taste was gone, she had to face facts: she was No One, about whom nobody cared. Nobody.

Hot tears filled her eyes. She ran to her bedroom, unlacing each of her new boots, and threw them as hard as she could against the wall. Then she flopped on her stomach, pressing her face into the braided rug. When the spot where she lay got too soggy with tears, she shifted to a new spot. Soon, she was right next to the bed. She raised her head, sniffling. In front of her, at face level, was her drawing. She yanked it out from under the bed and unrolled it in her lap. What a Dumb Dora she'd been to spend all that time on it. She took one last look at the

Bunny she'd drawn smack in the center of the picture. Good-bye to all that.

With a deep, ragged breath, she sat back on her heels. Slowly, she ripped off one long strip. Then another. And another. She tore the strips into postage-stamp-sized bits. Tore those bits in half. And half again. Afterward, she gathered up every scrap and threw the whole wretched mess into the fire. The flames blazed blue as the waxy color from the Crayolas fueled them. She felt as if she were watching her dearest dreams burn up right in front of her.

Someone rapped at her bedroom door.

Bunny jumped.

"May I come in?" It was Father.

"Yes, sir." Bunny hurried to remove her pinafore from the rocking chair, then opened the door for him. He entered, newspaper tucked under his arm, and took the recently cleared-off seat. She waited, a short step away from the chair.

"I think you owe your mother and sister an apology for your behavior at the dinner table."

Bunny leaned on the arm of the rocker. "But, Father, it's not fair—"

He held up a finger. "Mr. Reyburn is a man of honor with a difficult task. He made the best decision he could."

Best? Bunny wanted to shout, but that would not be proper at all. She took a deep breath and tried again to set forth her case. "But wouldn't the best decision be to select the best speaker?" Bunny had even caught Mrs.

Newcomb yawning when Belle practiced her speech in front of all the girls.

Father frowned. "Now, Bun. None of that. At any rate, you agreed to be part of the Welcome Committee, and you shall do just that. And do your best, no matter what your role. A Harnden's word must mean something."

Bunny shifted back and forth on her stocking feet. It was all very well for Father to say such things. He was the darling of Fifth Avenue. Everyone knew him and thought he was wonderful. He had no idea what it was like to be nobody. To be invisible.

"You'll do that for me?" he asked.

She fought back a sniffle. "I will."

Father pushed his glasses up on his handsome nose. "All right, then. Mother is sending Nanny up to"—he waved his hands around uncertainly—"to do something with your hair." He stood. "We'll make quite the pair to-morrow, you in your ringlets and petticoats and me in my morning coat."

Bunny bit back a complaint. Curls meant sleeping on rags. And starched petticoats made her legs itch. City Hall no longer held a promise of triumph, but a sense of doom. Yet she nodded in solemn agreement. She was a Harnden, after all.

"Good." Father handed her the newspaper he'd brought in with him. "You might enjoy the article in here about the ceremony."

Bunny took the paper.

Father chucked her under the chin. "Cheer up! Maybe

fashions will change by the time you're sixteen and instead of coming-out teas, it will be all the rage for the debutantes to make speeches. And you'll have yours all ready to go." He laughed at his joke, then glanced at his pocket watch. "Sleep well, Bunny." He leaned over and kissed the top of her head.

After he left, Bunny changed into her nightclothes, and presently Nanny appeared with the basket of rags and the special concoction to help hold the curl. The goo smelled like Nanny's liniment medicine. But all the juice had gone out of Bunny and she endured the torture quietly.

"Won't you be the charmer tomorrow," Nanny said, slathering on the goo.

A thought crashed like thunder in Bunny's head. "Winnifred's not coming, is she?"

The Princess herself, passing in the hall, answered the question. "I will be much too busy writing out invitations in my best hand." She swished through the doorway. "As if I would attend any function you are at," she added, in a whisper loud enough for Bunny to hear but too soft for Nanny's old ears. She twirled out of the room.

Bunny stuck her tongue out at Win's retreating back.

"Now, now, Miss Bunny," Nanny chided. "That's not the way to treat your sister."

If only Nanny knew. Bunny sat perfectly still, patiently allowing the last two hanks of hair to be slathered with glop and twirled onto a rag. Then she stood up, stretching. "Thank you, Nanny," she said, mindful of her manners. She kissed the old lady on her wrinkly cheek. "Good night."

"You are the one, aren't you?" Nanny said with a bemused smile.

Bunny wasn't sure what Nanny meant by that. No matter. She was soon asleep and dreaming of horrible fates befalling one Belle Wyatt Roosevelt.

Revenge

In the drowsy not-quite-awake moments before Nanny came to pull the drapes the next morning, Bunny remembered the paper Father had left for her to read. She skittered across the cold floor to snatch it from the rocker's seat. Quick as could be, she was back in bed, scootching around to find the lovely warm spot she'd recently vacated.

It wasn't Father's *New York Times*, but the *Town Topics*, Mother's "bible." Mother read it faithfully, always on the lookout for mention of their family. Bunny ran her finger up one column and down another, trying to find the article mentioning the ceremony at City Hall. Her finger stopped and she read aloud:

Little Envoys Arrive in Town

Mayor Jimmy Walker will greet some charming but very quiet ambassadors from the Land of the Sun.

Five exquisite Japanese dolls are visiting our fair city.

On hand for the ceremony will be Acting Consul General Uchiyama, special envoy Mr. Sekiya, Dr. Sidney Gulick, and Fifth Avenoodle Favorite Mr. Edward Walker Harnden. Belle Wyatt Roosevelt, daughter of Mr. and Mrs. Kermit Roosevelt, will participate in the presentation ceremony.

Bunny tossed the paper aside. No mention of the Welcome Committee. Just Belle Roosevelt. Always Belle. She wondered what the newspapers would say if they knew about the real Belle. The one who had backed Bunny into a corner after school and, like the snake she was, hissed in her face, "Good luck with your speech. Because you are going to need it." Then she'd stomped on Bunny's new white boots, for good measure. Bunny had never said a word to anyone about it. And look where that honorable action had gotten her!

Nanny brought in a breakfast tray. While Bunny poked at the grapefruit sections and scrambled eggs, a wobbly weed of a thought sprouted. Belle was no orator. She would flub up in some way. It would take only the teeniest-tiniest bit of effort on Bunny's part to help Belle embarrass herself thoroughly. Bunny's mind began to whir so that she forgot about her breakfast.

"Do you have the wibble-wobbles about today?" Nanny asked when she saw Bunny's uneaten breakfast. "Meeting the mayor. My, my." She forked up a bit of scrambled egg and held it to Bunny's lips. "One little bite for old Nanny?"

Bunny opened her mouth, took the offered bite, and chewed thoughtfully. Something would come to her. If only it were spring, rather than January. Then she could pull her famous frog-in-the-pinafore trick. That had turned Win's last birthday party into a free-for-all of screaming girls. Bunny smiled to remember it. One of her finest moments.

"Come on, dearie." Nanny nudged her out of her reverie and her bed. "Time to meet the day." Soon Bunny was wearing her best woolen dress, white stockings with a black garter above each knee, and black dress shoes with straps that buckled at the ankle. Nanny carefully combed each ringlet around her knobby fingers until eight fat brown sausages bounced around Bunny's head.

"Hold still, lovey." Nanny fussed and fumbled and finally fastened an enormous satin bow above Bunny's left ear. This fashion made Bunny feel like some kind of gift package, but it was the latest fad for girls her age, and heaven forbid if Mother didn't dress her daughters in the current fashion. Bunny did a little twirl for Nanny, who clapped her hands. "You look like a porcelain doll. Prettier than those Japanese ones, I'm sure."

Even Mother approved, in her own way, when she stopped Bunny in the entryway to give her fingernails an inspection. "Remember, Bunny, pretty is as pretty does."

"Yes, Mother." Bunny curtsied.

"Father will be down in a moment. Wait for him in

26

the library." Mother gave her a quick hug, then adjusted the satin hair bow. "There. Now, I must find Winnifred." She hurried off.

Bunny waited in Father's library as directed. Three steps into the room, her eye fell on Father's boyhood marble collection. The answer to her troubles was virtually under her nose! Quick as a wink, she snatched up one of the biggest aggies in the enormous glass jar. She was confident she would be able to find exactly the right moment to drop it during the ceremony. The clatter would freeze Belle's stiff words to the roof of her mouth. Then Bunny *would* have to step forward to save the day with her prettily prepared speech. Bunny was stunned by her own cleverness.

"Ready?" Father stood in the doorway.

"Yes, Father." Bunny smoothed her fur-trimmed wrapper. "Quite ready."

Soon, they were in the backseat of the new Town Car, purring their way down Fifth Avenue.

"Best view in the world, right, Bunny?" Father tapped on the rear passenger window as they angled off onto Broadway, just past Madison Square Garden. Bunny nodded agreement, her nose pressed against the glass. It was like having her own silent film rolling in front of her—all the colors and automobiles and pushcarts and people. And so many of those people reading the paper as they went about their business. Just think, tomorrow they'd all be reading about her! Not Belle Roosevelt. She smiled.

Bunny craned her neck as they rolled past the Scribner

Building, where Father had taken her once to meet an editor friend of his. They'd had lunch near there, at that delicatessen, where Father had let her drink an egg cream with her sandwich. When Scribner's edged out of sight, she turned the other way to look for the spires of First Presbyterian Church, where they attended services on Sundays. Thinking of church and Reverend Speers' last sermon made Bunny squirm a bit on the seat. His lecture about "pride goeth before a fall" and Mother's admonition that "pretty is as pretty does" were almost enough to dissuade her from her course of action.

Then she remembered the worst thing—when Belle had written Bunny's name in her spite book. That had been the kiss of death. No one at Mrs. Newcomb's had dared befriend Bunny after that. It was all because of Belle that Bunny's school days were lonely and long.

She felt for the aggie in her pocket. Still there. Now all she had to do was find the right moment to use it.

"Mayor Walker," Father was saying, "allow me to present my youngest. Genevieve, this is His Honor, the mayor."

Bunny curtsied and Mayor Walker patted her on the head. He smelled of cigars and something like Nanny's cough medicine. "The mirror image of your charming wife," the mayor said, clapping Father on the back. "If I might have a word?"

"Can you find your friends, Bunny?" Father asked as he strode with the mayor through a small door to the right of the reception room. He didn't wait for her reply.

Father always had to be early. "Ten minutes ahead of time is late," he said. So Bunny had arrived well before the rest of the Welcome Committee. Including Belle Roosevelt.

The French doors to the reception room were ajar. Bunny nudged them a bit farther apart and squirmed through. Her stomach was reminding her that she had only picked at her breakfast. Perhaps the cookies and punch were already set out and she could have some before anyone else.

The long, linen-draped tables were empty of refreshments, but Bunny wandered into the room anyway, attracted by the lectern opposite her. Glancing around to make sure she was alone, Bunny made her way there. With great poise, she stood behind it, imagining the room positively bulging with distinguished guests. She began to say her speech.

✳

Well, this little one is certainly full of herself. I watch her declaim and gesture. It seems as if she thinks the spotlight shines on her, and her alone, and as if that were the way it should be. *Such vanity is most unbecoming.* I note to my sisters.

Her speech is pretty, Miss Japan counters, and my other sisters agree.

It is not bad, I concede, after listening a bit longer. *But even a perfect pear can harbor a worm within.*

Miss Japan makes no reply to my wise observation. Odd; she generally has something to say on every subject.

Bunny finished her speech, and as the last syllable died away, she curtsied, almost certain she could hear applause.

Wait. There was no *almost*. Bunny's eyes darted around the still-semidarkened room. The sound was faint, but it was definitely applause. Where was it coming from? She listened harder. From her left, behind her.

She whirled around, peeking behind a painted silk screen to come face to face with five Japanese dolls, each about the size of her four-year-old cousin. Bunny stared intently. Five pairs of hands rested on five silk kimonos. Of course. They were just dolls! Had she expected them to be clapping?

She peeked under the draped table to see if someone was hiding there. It'd be so like Mary Louise Miller to play this kind of trick! She was probably waiting for the right moment to pop out and startle Bunny.

No one was under the table. Bunny let the table skirt drop.

She must be light-headed from lack of food, and it was making her hear things. That was the only possible explanation.

As she straightened up, her eye fell on the doll wearing an orange kimono sprayed with pale blue flowers. Chrysanthemums. Leaning against her was a pint-sized silk parasol, adorned with a single chrysanthemum. Bunny looked down the row of dolls. Each had its own parasol, as well as numerous travel essentials: fans, tea sets, a spare pair of sandals—too many accessories to take in. Bunny moved toward the doll in orange silk, scarcely aware of the four others on the table.

A creamy white card rested in a stand at the doll's sandaled feet. "Miss Kana-gawa," Bunny pronounced slowly. "That's a tongue twister." She smiled at her own little joke, but one look at the doll and her smile quickly faded. She couldn't explain it, but she felt as if the doll was looking straight at her. "You're just a doll," she said.

No answer came.

Bunny felt in her pocket for the aggie. The commotion it would make on this slick floor—she smiled again to think of it. What about a quick test run? She pulled out the marble and knelt down, holding it mere inches from the floor. Bunny held her breath and let it drop. Even from that height, the clatter was sufficiently and deliciously loud. She stood, repocketing her prize.

Upright again, she found her eyes drawn back to the doll's. Fringed with dark lashes, they were as dark as the bark of the elm trees lining Bunny's street. But it wasn't simply the color—so different from her own green eyes— that caught her. It was silly, really. This was a doll, after all! But Bunny couldn't avoid the look of disapproval in those eyes. It was almost as if the doll knew what she had planned. Bunny stuck her tongue out. So there!

The doll glared back. Bunny stepped closer. Two could play at this game. "Mother says 'pretty is as pretty does,'" she told the doll. "Maybe they don't teach that where you come from." She lifted her head, imitating Winnifred's told-you-so manner.

This time when she looked at the doll, she saw something else in those eyes, something that felt unpleasantly familiar.

✳

Well, this child is pretty enough, though I much prefer my silky straight hair to those horrible curls. And I can see that her hands are clean. A small blessing.

I gaze back at the child and catch her in the act of sticking out her tongue. Little wretch!

Hmm. Those green eyes of hers are intriguing. The color of a rice paddy in the early spring. As I study those round American eyes, I see something else veiled behind the boldness and conceit.

Miss Japan, look at that girl's eyes. Tell me what you see.
I see spring rice fields.

I can sense Miss Japan's impatience.

But it matters not what I see. It is what you see that is important.

I continue to study the girl. How odd that Miss Japan, usually so perceptive, can't see what I do: loneliness. A vision, like a painting on a silk fan, unfolds in the air in front of me. A vision of this child—at school, at play, at home—with others around her, but always alone.

✳

The Best-Laid Plans

It was almost as if the doll's eyes were the two lenses of a stereoscope, only instead of a scene from a European cathedral, Bunny saw a scene from school. One that had happened the other day in the cloakroom. The girls were hanging up their things after a nature walk in Central Park. Mean-spirited Clemmy Moore was buzzing around, making her usual stinging comments. She fluttered in front of Belle. "So how is your father doing in the hospital, dear Belle?"

Bunny's coat hook was next to Belle's. She couldn't help but notice the stricken look on Belle's face. The look passed quickly and Belle's face was once again unreadable. "He's much better, thank you," she answered tightly.

"Father says it's such a shame." Clemmy fluffed her curls in the cloakroom mirror. "But then, many weak men can't handle their drink."

Bunny was stunned. Certainly there had been rumors around town about Belle's father. But to throw them up at her, here, in front of all the other girls . . . Bunny wouldn't have thought even Clemmy could sink so low. Without thinking, Bunny placed her hand on Belle's arm. "Don't listen to her."

Belle didn't move for a second. Then she turned. "Please remove your hand," she'd said, shaking Bunny off. "I don't need any help from a Dumb Dora like you." She'd turned on the toes of her perfect white boots and stomped back into the classroom.

It was so like Belle, Bunny hadn't given the episode another thought.

Until now. Why would she think of it now?

✳

I feel a twinge inside my muslin chest, under the left side of my kimono. Since the day I was created, I have never had a moment of feeling unwell. What is causing this pain now?

I have heard it does hurt a bit, Miss Japan comforts me.

What does? I ask.

Being awakened.

What do I do to make it stop?

But Miss Japan gives no answer.

The ache in my chest makes me feel so strange. Snippets of Master Tatsuhiko's words swirl in my head. "Bad and good are intertwined with one rope," I remember him saying once. This feeling inside me is certainly bad. What good can be intertwined with it?

Other words I had heard from Master Tatsuhiko come to mind. Sayings like "One kind word can warm three winter months" and "Spilt water will not return to the tray." All of it was as clear to me as a bowl of mud then, and is no clearer now.

I turn my attention back to the girl, who is looking at me intently. My gaze in return is equally intent.

✳

Bunny stared at the Miss Kanagawa doll. Its eyes were as still as a steamy New York summer night. She looked into the eyes of each of the other four dolls. Nothing.

This was so silly. They were dolls. Nothing more. Bunny's imagination was running away with her. Perhaps she should go find Father.

But something drew her back to the end of the table. To Miss Kanagawa. She reached out to stroke orange silk, her fingers hovering inches from the gown.

"Oh, there you are." It was Mary Louise Miller. "Mr. Reyburn says we must all wait in the mayor's office."

Bunny dropped her arm but otherwise didn't move.

"Come on!" Mary Louise tugged at her sleeve.

With a lingering backward glance, Bunny followed Mary Louise. But her thoughts were still inside the reception room. With Miss Kanagawa.

"Ready, Bunny? Mary Louise? Let's find the other girls." Mr. Reyburn bustled over, gathering up the members of the Welcome Committee. It wasn't until he lined them up that Bunny realized she was standing next to Belle. Thoughts about the doll quickly vanished. This was perfect for her plan!

But then something jabbed her in the chest. She had the sensation of being poked by an umbrella. No, not an umbrella. Something less pointy. More like the end of a parasol.

Absurd.

Bunny shook herself.

"Stand still, won't you?" Belle said. Her voice sounded parched and thin.

Bunny started to say something snippy in return. Then she caught sight of a perfect pearl-sized tear rolling out

35

from under Belle's eyelid and down her cheek. Belle? Crying?

"Are you all right?" Bunny asked.

Belle bit her lip, shaking her head no. "I'm going to make an awful mess of it," she said. "I wish they hadn't chosen me."

I wish they hadn't chosen you, either, Bunny thought. She fingered the marble in her pocket.

✳

Our actions make the fragrance of our lives.

✳

Bunny's head snapped left, then right. Where had that voice come from? Oh, why hadn't she eaten breakfast? Bunny shook her head to clear it. What was going on?

"It's time." Mr. Reyburn cued the string quartet. The girls peeked out of the mayor's office to watch the dignitaries file into the reception room. The screen had been set aside and there the dolls were, in full view of everyone. When the girls were given the signal to enter the reception room themselves, Bunny focused her gaze on the mayor, who was stepping up to the podium.

✳

Would you smell of plums? Or vinegar?

✳

Bunny glanced behind her. No one else seemed to hear anything. All eyes were intent on the mayor.

Bunny discreetly tapped at her left ear. Where was this voice coming from? And what did it mean? She saw the mayor gesture right to the special envoy and then left to the dolls. But nothing he said was penetrating through the strange words in her head.

The quartet launched into another piece. Bunny quietly cleared her throat, as if that would clear the puzzling thoughts.

❋

Well? What will you choose?

❋

Bunny tossed her head like an impatient horse.

"Stand still," Mary Louise hissed. "What on earth is wrong with you?"

"Sorry." Bunny gave her head one last stealthy shake.

There, that seemed to do the trick. Now the only thing she heard was the quartet playing the first notes of the American national anthem. Bunny relaxed. Smiled. Stood a little taller. When the music quavered to a close, Mr. Sekiya, the special envoy traveling with the dolls, stepped to the podium and began to speak.

Bunny's hand slipped into her pocket, reaching for the smooth, cool marble. She glanced right. Belle was as pale as Mother's best Irish linen. She looked as stricken as she had that day in the cloakroom.

As if she hadn't a friend on this earth.

Bunny did want to be noticed. But not for smelling like vinegar. She unpocketed her hand and put it on Belle's arm. This time, Belle did not shake it off.

"You're going to be wonderful," Bunny whispered.

Belle looked at her in surprise.

Bunny nodded so hard all eight ringlets bounced around her head. She heard Belle take a deep breath as Mr. Reyburn waved her forward. "And here to accept Miss Japan on behalf of the children of New York City is Miss Belle Wyatt Roosevelt."

Belle hesitated for an instant.

"You're a Roosevelt," Bunny whispered again. "Charge!"

Belle stepped forward and gave her little speech. It wasn't as clever as Bunny's, but she said it nicely and only stumbled once. When she finished, she glanced Bunny's way with a shy smile that softened her sharp face. She looked almost friendly. Bunny smiled back.

Then a trumpet sounded and the musicians launched into the Japanese national anthem. During the majestic march, Mr. Sekiya moved solemnly over to the tables where the Ambassadors of Friendship were on display. He bowed three times to the dolls and said something in Japanese. Then he gently and carefully lifted Miss Japan off the table. He turned and slowly made his way across the shiny marble floor to Belle. When he was in front of her, he bowed to her as well. She curtsied and reached out her arms for Miss Japan. He handed her the doll.

It must've been heavier than Belle expected, because

it wobbled in her arms. Then she wobbled. A sharp gasp came from the row of dignitaries. The mayor rose halfway to his feet.

In an instant, Bunny whisked to Belle's side, helping to hold the doll until Belle could get a firm grasp. The room burst into applause as Bunny stepped back in line, ducking her head shyly. Bunny caught sight of Father, who gave her a little salute. She realized that the unpleasant poking sensation had disappeared. She felt light. Happy. And proud. As proud as if she'd given a speech herself.

After the ceremony, after all the compliments from the adults and the other Welcome Committee girls, Bunny made her way to the table where the remaining dolls stood. She stopped in front of Miss Kanagawa, staring into her eyes. This time, she heard nothing. Saw nothing.

How silly to expect anything different! She was only a doll, after all.

But still . . .

For ten days, all five dolls were on display at Lord & Taylor. They attracted crowds of admirers, of all ages, which pleased Mr. Reyburn no end because most of the visitors also purchased something from his store. Many came to call more than once. A ladies' lunch group so enjoyed the dolls that they returned on the weekend with their families in tow. A local doll collectors' association paid their respects no fewer than three times in order to fully appreciate not only the dolls but also the *accoutrement* that accompanied them. The association members disagreed amiably among themselves about which were more charming—the painted silk parasols, the diminutive tea sets, or the lacquered kimono boxes.

None of the visitors, however, signed the guest book more often than one eleven-year-old girl who cajoled her nanny into taking her to call each day of the dolls' short stay in the city. Once, Bunny bumped into Belle Roosevelt, also visiting the dolls. Bunny had heard from Mary Louise that her name had been removed from Belle's spite book. But at the store, Belle only nodded at Bunny and went on her way.

Every afternoon, Bunny paid her respects to Miss Kanagawa while Nanny eased her bunions in the tearoom. And every afternoon, Bunny waited for another message from the doll. But nothing came, not even one whispered word.

On the last day of the dolls' engagement at Lord & Taylor, Bunny was more like a snail than like her bouncy namesake. "I've never seen such a child!" exclaimed Nanny. "First you bustle me along the streets like there's a fire, then you dawdle as if you're headed for a spanking." Nanny shook her head. "You are a puzzle." She took off her gloves in the department store's vestibule. "Shall I stand with you?"

"No!" Bunny's answer came out more sharply than she intended. "No, thank you, Nanny. I'll meet you in the tearoom when I'm done."

Nanny glanced at her bodice watch. "Four o'clock?"

"Yes, ma'am." Bunny nodded, then hurried off to the dolls' display.

This crowd was the smallest yet. Most of the city's residents had already been to gawk at these wonders of Japanese artistry. Bunny was glad, really, that it was a quieter day. Fewer visitors meant she could get closer to the dolls. Well, closer to Miss Kanagawa. Still, she had to hug the edges of the room for a good long while, waiting for the right moment, until there was no one around.

Bunny was good at speeches. But when it came to finding the words on this day, it was more difficult than sitting through one of Reverend Speers' Sunday sermons. Silly, too, were the tears stinging the back of her eyes, threatening to pop out and roll down her cheeks in a childish display of emotion. She was much too old for this piffling business of dolls.

And yet. Here she was, tearing up at the thought of this good-bye. Ridiculous.

A newly installed placard explained that the dolls would be sent, in groups of six, to various parts of the country; the Friendship Doll Committee hadn't yet decided where. Only Miss Japan's traveling days were over. She was going to the National Museum in Washington, D.C., her new permanent home.

When Bunny finished reading all these details, she found herself alone in the room. Now was her chance.

She cleared her throat. "Do you remember when we first met?" She looked to see if Miss Kanagawa responded.

Those dark eyes stared straight ahead. "You seemed so haughty and standoffish." Bunny grinned a wobbly grin. "Well, I don't think I was so charming myself. But you did something to me that day. I don't know how. I truly don't. And maybe I made it all up, because you haven't spoken to me since." Bunny put her hands in her pockets. "Father said his buttons popped right off his vest when I came to the rescue, he was so proud. Mother can't stop telling all her friends about it. And Winnifred has written my name back on the coming-out tea guest list." Bunny rolled her eyes. "Not that that's any great prize."

Bunny thought that remark might get a tiny reaction from her quiet friend. But no.

"I couldn't have done it without you. So I wanted to give you this." Bunny pulled something from her right pocket, and then set it inside the doll-sized steamer trunk that rested at Miss Kanagawa's feet.

"Good-bye." Bunny bowed, three times, to the doll, as she had seen Mr. Sekiya do.

"Bunny! Oh, there you are!" Nanny bustled over. "I nearly had apoplexy. You were to meet me at four! And now it's nearly a quarter past the hour." Nanny's wrinkled cheeks flared pink with worry.

"I'm so sorry, Nanny. I lost track of time." Bunny hugged the old lady. "I'm ready now." She twined her arm through Nanny's and they made their way to the front of the store. Bunny didn't glance back. She didn't dare. It was the only way to keep from blubbering.

Lord & Taylor's front doors closed promptly at five

p.m. Shortly after, a specially hired crew appeared to pack up Miss Japan and her six companions. Each accessory— from black lacquer fan case to tea tin—was carefully wrapped in cotton batting. After each doll's possessions were cared for, then began the process of placing doll and belongings in the trunk, like fitting together a jigsaw puzzle.

"What's this?" asked the frizzy-haired woman in charge of Miss Kanagawa.

"Looks like a marble," said one of the other packing committee members.

"Shall I remove it?" asked Frizzy Hair.

"If it's in the trunk, it must belong there," said a third packer.

Miss Kanagawa felt herself lifted off the stand she'd rested on for ten long days. Gently, she was wrapped in muslin and placed in her trunk. The lid closed, locks setting with a double click. In the dark, Miss Kanagawa felt something resting under her graceful hand. It was round and smooth and polished.

As she lay there, a dull ache pulsed under the left side of her orange silk kimono, like a toothache.

Or a heartbeat.

Middles

In the middle of difficulty lies opportunity.

—ALBERT EINSTEIN

MUSEUM TO AUCTION ITEMS

**Making room for a New and
Exciting Focus, says Board
President**

CHICAGO, MAR. 30, 1933 (AP) —
The Wrobel Museum of Illinois History has a new leader with a fresh
vision.

"We're very pleased that the
museum and its exhibits will be returning to a focus on state history,"
said Mrs. Marvin George, museum
board president. She declined to

45

comment further, promising that more information would be made available next month.

In the meantime, in order to make room for new acquisitions and exhibits, the museum will be auctioning off surplus items. One of the objects headed for the auction block is a doll sent to the children of this country by Japanese schoolchildren in 1927.

✳

MISS KANAGAWA

Not that I would ever grumble, but these Americans have strange ways of treating an honored guest. When we first arrived, my sisters and I were feted and celebrated. The parties! The crowds of admirers! The photographers and reporters!

After touring the country for a time, we went our separate ways, to museums. At first, so many people wanted to pay their respects that visitors were required to make appointments. Then, like the water in a late summer stream, the public's interest waned. One day, no appointments were needed, and some time after that—I have no idea how long it was because time passes much differently for a doll than it does for a human—I was rudely removed from my display and once again closed up in my trunk with all my belongings.

Ah, well. It is restful in here, wrapped not only in muslin and cotton batt but in warm memories. I cannot help but think of the girl with eyes the color of rice fields in early spring. That little scamp.

I saw right through her, snip-snap, and those plans of hers to ruin the moment for the other girl. Why I bothered about such affairs, I have no idea. I was created for bigger things, after all. Miss Japan was the one always going on and on about opening one's heart. Oddly, my elder sister could not see beyond that girl's bright green eyes to the cloud of loneliness beneath. It was up to me to be of service, trusted emissary that I am. Thanks to me, that girl could not carry through her wicked deed.

What's that noise? Could it be? Oh, yes! The lid of my trunk is now opening. The light! It will feel heavenly to see again after this long, dark rest.

Ooof! That clumsy oaf needs to take more care in setting me on my feet. Doesn't he realize I've been cooped up for ages?

My goodness. What a lot of dolls! None as attractive as me, of course.

A roly-poly baby doll greets me: *Another visitor from another land. Welcome.*

Master Tatsuhiko would have shuddered to see this doll— a toy, really with a button on her stomach that a child could push to make the doll clap her hands. How unrefined!

Ah, mon amie, *I completely agree with you.* A slim Bleuette doll in a black beret and red velvet cloak is standing to my right. *Some people have such odd ideas about dolls. They think us mere playthings.*

I remember this from my Waking Time before. There were children who had come to the museum to see me and were quite dismayed to learn they could not undress me or comb

47

my hair. *It is my job to accept strange customs,* I explain to the Bleuette doll, who lets me know her name is Brigitte and that she is from France. *I am an ambassador. An Ambassador of Friendship from Japan.*

Ooh-la-la. It is an honor, Madame. I am at your service.

Now that my eyes are adjusting to the light, I can see I am in a vast room filled with dolls of every shape and variety. Some have been modeled after children, and some after animals, like that elephant and brown bear in the far corner. Some are elegant, like myself and my French friend, but others are nothing more than bits of yarn and muslin, like that raggedy brother-and-sister pair with the unruly red hair and striped stockings. And there are some dolls made simply from paper. It is amazing. Astonishing.

Brigitte, what is this place? There are so many of us.

That I do not know. But, alors, *here comes the bearded man. He is the one who has brought us all here.* Brigitte has alerted me to a portly figure, puffing into the room, carrying an armful of doll stands. He is speaking to a younger, slimmer man.

※

"I tell you," he says, "even at ten cents a head, we'll make a fortune with this exhibit. They say that over one million people will attend the fair. Think of it! One million." The bearded man stops to pat his forehead with a dingy handkerchief.

"I sure hope so, Pop. With so many people out of work,

though . . ." The younger man's voice is tinged with doubt.

"This Depression is all the more reason for people to come! You watch. They're hungry for something bright, something shiny. And this Chicago World's Fair is just the ticket." The bearded man stuffs his handkerchief into his back pocket. "Come on, we've got another shipping crate to unload." They bustle out of the room.

✳

A World's Fair! That sounds important, very important indeed. That's why I was sent here. Greeting visitors from all the world over will be an enormous responsibility. I look around the room again. It is no wonder the bearded man enlisted my help. With such a ragtag collection, he is going to need it.

✳

Downers Grove, Illinois — 1933

Lois Brown

March

Lois Brown was five minutes older than her best friend, Mabel Hedquist, and five times more reckless. She'd chipped a front tooth sailing off the banister at age six and wore a dashing scar over her left eye from soaring off the swings into the wild blue yonder in third grade. Now she lay in a heap on the ground, certain some of her parts weren't working right.

Mabel and her younger brother Johnny came running over. "Is anything broken?" Johnny asked.

Lois closed her eyes. "My shoulder feels funny."

"You don't look very good," said Mabel. She knelt next to her friend, her own face as white as the milk in the bottles on the neighbor's porch. "Johnny, go get Mrs. Brown. I'll wait here."

Johnny's bare feet flew across the vacant lot and toward the Brown home.

Lois opened her eyes, managing a weak smile. "I was flying there. For a second."

Mabel shook her head. "I knew this wasn't a good idea." She glanced up at the barn roof where her friend had been perched a few moments ago.

"I need a bigger umbrella, that's all." Lois closed her eyes again.

Dad actually laughed at supper that night when Mom told him what had happened. "She's a Brown, all right," he said. "Like a hound on a scent. Gets her mind set on something and tracks it down."

Mom clucked her tongue. "Howard, don't you give her one ounce of encouragement. The doctor said she was lucky it was only her collarbone broken. It could've been her neck! Next time—"

"The good thing about breaking a collarbone," Lois interjected, "is that there isn't much for the doctor to do." That hadn't been the case when she'd needed her forehead stitched up. That time, the doctor said there wasn't another child in Downers Grove that he'd patched up as much as he had Lois. She took that as a compliment. Not Mom. Since there wasn't much that could be done for a broken collarbone except let it heal, Mom rigged up a sling with an old scarf to help keep the bone in place.

"There is nothing good about breaking a bone, no

matter what kind it is," Mom said. "This fixation on fly-ing has got to stop. You are no Amelia Earhart! The next time you pull a stunt like this, I'll make sure you don't sit down for a week. You listen to me, now."

"Yes, Mom." Lois finished her scalloped potatoes. "May I please be excused?"

"You may." Dad took another biscuit.

"To your room," Mom said.

"But—" Lois had hoped to go across the street to Mabel's to show off the sling.

"No buts. I think you need some time to consider your rash actions." Mom folded her arms across her apron. When she did that, no amount of wheedling would work. Lois awkwardly carried her plate to the sink and trudged to her room.

She eased on top of her chenille bedspread, trying to find a pain-free position. Gazing up at the ceiling, she studied the magazine pictures she'd thumbtacked there—Charles Lindbergh and Wiley Post, sure, but lady fliers, too, like Amelia Earhart, Bessie Coleman, and Florence "Pancho" Barnes. And she imagined herself in every photo, in each pilot's place—standing next to *The Spirit of St. Louis*, climbing into the cockpit of Amelia's *Canary*, bringing Wiley Post's *Winnie Mae* in for a landing. It wasn't that much of a stretch for Lois to dream of being a pilot. There were lots of women aviators! But it took money to learn to fly. Lots of it. And money was in awfully short supply in the Brown household.

Lois shifted her arm so her shoulder didn't ache as much. One day, she would soar through the clouds. She would. No matter how long it took.

April

Lois knew her mother was upset the minute she stepped into the kitchen after school. And it wasn't simply because Great-aunt Eunice was sitting at the table across from her, tapping her walking stick on the floor and complaining about Mom's watery coffee. The two telltale spots of pink on Mom's face were a sure sign she was peeved.

Lois closed the back door quietly behind her. For one brief moment, she thought Aunt Eunice might not pay her any mind. She tiptoed across the black and white linoleum tiles.

"I see your arm is healed up. I certainly hope it doesn't end up shorter than the other one. Heaven knows where you get such ideas. Flying!" Aunt Eunice helped herself to another cookie from Mom's Blue Willow plate. "In my day, girls weren't allowed to run wild like little hooligans." She finished the cookie, then held out her age-spotted hand. "Wasn't today spelling test day? Where is your paper?"

Lois glanced at Mom, who gave her a best-do-as-she-says nod. She unbuckled the straps of her book bag and slid the test out, presenting it to Aunt Eunice.

She looked down her nose at it. "Ninety-nine percent." Her wrinkly mouth puckered up even more, like she'd bit into a sour apple. "Study harder next time." She waved the test at Lois as if it were a dead mouse.

"Yes, ma'am." Lois took the paper and started for her room again.

"I don't recall dismissing you." The kitchen chair creaked as Aunt Eunice shifted forward. "Ellie, you must teach this child some manners."

The pink spots on Mom's cheeks glowed brighter. She held out her arms to Lois, who stepped into the comfort of her mother's embrace.

"Let's see your hands."

Lois hesitated.

"Hands," repeated Aunt Eunice.

Slowly, Lois held them out.

"Still biting your nails, I see." Aunt Eunice seemed almost pleased to find this additional flaw.

"May I be excused, Mom? I have homework." That was a fib, but Lois was desperate to escape Aunt Eunice's scrutiny. Next would be a comment that Lois' hair was too curly or some such, but sooner or later Aunt Eunice would shift her arrows from Lois to Dad.

Today, though, Aunt Eunice went straight from the bitten nails to Dad. "I suppose it's too much to hope that your husband has found work."

"Howard is this very day exploring an opportunity in Joliet." Mom stood up and stepped over to the stove. "More coffee, Eunice?" She picked up the percolator.

Aunt Eunice held her hand over her cup. "No. No more." She took another cookie—the last. Jeepers! Talk about needing to learn some manners! "Today's men simply don't know how to apply themselves. My Milton worked every day of his life."

Lois wished she had a nickel for every time she'd heard about Uncle Milton being such a hard worker. Dad said he worked that hard because he never wanted to be at home with Aunt Eunice. Mom had laughed when Dad said that, but then had scolded him. "Howard—she's family."

Lois didn't know how Mom could keep her thoughts to herself when Aunt Eunice started in on Dad. It whittled at Lois' heart to watch him grow quieter and quieter each day he was out of work. He was a crackerjack mechanic. But he'd fixed every car and tractor in town that needed fixing. This morning, he'd hitched a ride to Joliet because he'd heard there might be a job there.

"May I be excused?" Lois asked again.

"Of course," Mom said.

"Not yet." Aunt Eunice brushed molasses-cookie crumbs from her fingers before reaching into her enormous pocketbook, from which she produced a colorful pamphlet. With a flourish, she deposited it on the table.

Lois couldn't help herself. The bright letters on the front cover commanded attention. She edged closer to get a better look. "The Chicago World's Fair: A Century of Progress." She'd heard about the fair—who hadn't? Mabel's cousin got a job there and he told Mabel it was like working in a Jules Verne novel, with something fantastic everywhere he turned.

"Education is more than simply sitting at a desk," Aunt

Eunice declared. Lois looked up at her, confused. "Experiences are also educational. And I have decided to expand your education, Lois, by taking you to the World's Fair."

Lois could hardly trust her ears. To go to the fair! With money as tight as it was, she hadn't even let herself dream about the possibility. Wait till she told Mabel! Then she stopped. Going to the fair with her great-aunt was another story.

"Isn't there something you want to say?" Aunt Eunice demanded.

"Th-thank you?" Lois stammered.

Aunt Eunice nodded. "You may keep the pamphlet. I thought we'd go on opening day. May twenty-seventh. We'll start out early. No need for breakfast. We'll dine at the Quaker Oats Pavilion. Ten cents for all the pancakes you can eat, cooked by Aunt Jemima herself."

"This is very generous of you, Eunice," Mom said. "Lois is so over the moon, she can hardly speak." She gave Lois a look that meant *Say something*.

Lois reached for the pamphlet, picked it up, and held it to her chest. "Thank you, Aunt Eunice. This is the best surprise ever."

Aunt Eunice adjusted her hat. "Very well, then. *Now*, you may be excused."

It was all Lois could do not to run to her bedroom. She forced herself to walk slowly and ladylike. She didn't want to do anything that would make Aunt Eunice change her mind about the offer. Even if it meant going with her

Lois grinned. "Roger and out." She read farther down the page. "Look what it says here. The ride costs twenty-five cents." She flipped the pamphlet closed. Her grin faded. "I guess that lets me out."

"If I had a quarter, I'd give it to you," Mabel said. "So you could ride across the sky."

Lois hugged her. "You're the best," she said.

When Lois and Mom sat down that night—without Dad—to plates of lima beans for the fourth night in a row, Lois couldn't eat. Her insides were plumb full of excitement about going to the fair.

"Did you know the Sky Ride towers are over six hundred feet tall?" Lois pushed a lima bean around her plate. "And the rocket cars are named after famous people?"

"They are?" Mom buttered a slice of bread and passed it to Lois.

Lois had been sitting on the pamphlet. She pulled it out. "Like Gracie Allen. And George Burns."

Mom got up to reheat the afternoon's coffee. "I wouldn't ride in any of those things, no matter who they're named after." She shivered. "You'd be so high, people on the ground would look like cabbage worms."

"I wouldn't mind that," said Lois. She remembered Mabel's advice and decided not to say anything more. But she couldn't stop thinking about it: soaring along like a bird, with clouds drifting by under your nose. Being able to see far beyond Chicago. Maybe even to Kalamazoo! Of course, the rocket cars were connected to the Sky Ride by cables, so it wouldn't be *exactly* like flying. But it would be closer to it than jumping off Swansons' barn with an umbrella!

She wondered if Aunt Eunice would think that the Sky Ride was educational, like the rest of the fair. That would be Lois' wish tonight, on the first evening star. "Do you think Dad will be home by bedtime?" she asked.

"You know he will be if he can." Mom poured herself some coffee. "Why don't you make him up a plate, just in case?"

Lois made up a plate, then helped Mom wash the dishes, finishing in time to listen to most of *Buck Rogers* on the radio. She read until eight-thirty. Dad still wasn't home, so she said her prayers with Mom, ending with "And God bless Dad. Help him find a job," before clambering into bed. After Mom kissed her and turned out the light, Lois thought about how many kids had prayed that same prayer tonight. Almost all of her schoolmates' fathers were out of work. And it was that way all over the state. All over the country! How would God ever answer that many prayers? She knew that she and Mom and Dad were luckier than most. They wouldn't lose their house. It was all paid for. And there were just the three of them. Not seven, like Mabel's family, with all those big, strapping, eternally hungry boys.

Besides, Mom was so clever at making do. The hole in the sole of Lois' oxfords was repaired with a thin piece of cardboard slipped inside the shoe. When the collar on Dad's good shirt started to look shabby, she snipped it off, turned it around, and sewed it back on with the ragged edge to the inside. And she could make five pounds of lima beans go farther than anyone in town.

Mom and Dad had made it an adventure the first year after the plant closed, finding ways to make ends meet. Lois wasn't bothered one bit to wear her boy cousins' hand-me-down overalls. And Mom's garden turned into jar after jar of canned food.

It was harder for Mabel's family. They lived in a boardinghouse and had no garden of their own. Every Saturday, Mabel, Elaine, and their mother got up in the wee hours to make doughnuts that Kenneth, the oldest, sold three for a dime at the train station. Her middle brother, Benjamin, delivered papers. And Johnny, the youngest, ran errands for the Dinwiddie sisters for nickels. Lois knew that President Franklin D. Roosevelt was working hard to help people get back to work, but she hoped he would hurry up a bit. It seemed that Mabel grew thinner every week.

Lois tiptoed to her window and watched for the stars to come out. She made her wish on the first one she saw. Then she tiptoed back to bed, where she added a prayer for Mabel's family. She dozed off and on, starting at every sound outside her window, thinking it might be Dad home from Joliet. She finally fell asleep and was wakened by the clinking of milk bottles on the front porch as the milkman made his deliveries.

After she heard the milkman's heavy boots tromp down the steps, she heard a lighter set of shoes skip up.

"Dad!" She threw back the covers and hurried downstairs to the kitchen as fast as she could.

"Pumpkin!" Dad scooped her up and swung her around, settling her onto a chair at the kitchen table. He settled onto the chair next to her.

"Thank you, Ellie." He took the cup of coffee Mom offered him, then smiled at Lois. "How did you manage on that spelling test without me here to quiz you?"

"Ninety-nine percent," Lois answered.

"Practically perfect! That's my girl." He toasted her with his coffee. Even though he was wearing a big smile, his eyes looked tired and his face was shadowed with stubble. And something else.

"Grease!" She rubbed at the splotch on his cheek. "Dad! You got a job."

Mom clapped her hands under her chin, as if she were praying. "You might have told me right off. Oh, Howard. A job!" She dabbed at her eyes with the hem of her apron.

"Well, it's temporary," Dad said.

"What is it?" Lois bounced on her chair. "Who are you working for?"

"Hansen's delivery service. Mr. Hansen has a fleet of ten trucks." Dad slurped his coffee, then grinned. "Lucky for me, each and every one of them is older than Henry Ford himself. They evidently break down on a regular basis."

"Well, then, don't fix them *too* good!" Lois said.

They all laughed. There would be no chance of Dad not knocking himself out to get each and every clunker up and running. "Browns always do their best" was the family motto.

"So that's my news." He tousled Lois' hair.

"Well, I have some swell news of my own!" Lois told him all about Aunt Eunice and the fair and the Sky Ride. "But I wish I were going with you and Mom," she finished.

"Ah, my girl." Dad grabbed her hands. "Never look a gift horse in the mouth. You go and chew up every bit of grand adventure that day has to offer."

Lois pictured herself traipsing at Aunt Eunice's side all over the fairgrounds, listening to her complain about this, that, and the other thing. How many times would she scold Lois for not staying close? How many times would she cluck her tongue in disapproval of something Mom and Dad had done? How many times would they have to sit and rest because Aunt Eunice's ankles had puffed out over her shoes, like a pair of toasted marshmallows? Lois sighed. But at least she would get to go. Not many other children in Downers Grove would be that lucky. Dad was right. Putting up with Aunt Eunice *was* a small price to pay for seeing the World's Fair.

✳

MISS KANAGAWA

The fair opens tomorrow and Mr. Beard is just now bringing in the last two dolls. Both cloth. One is dressed as a Red Cross worker and one as a character named Alice in Wonderland.

We are Madame Alexander dolls, the Red Cross doll announces.

The best is saved for the last, her friend adds.

Madame Alexander dolls indeed! Imagine being so full of

oneself! Humph. I can't help feeling like the cat that got the cream, however, because when Mr. Beard finished arranging us all, I was given the best spot in the exhibit: apart from the others, as is only proper, with a single spotlight showing off my *gofun* face, my graceful hands, and, of course, my elegant kimono. Mr. Beard's gangly son hand-lettered the placards accompanying each display. He read aloud what he had written for mine: "Madame Ambassador. Admire here a doll handmade by a master Japanese doll-maker, dressed in exquisite silk and crowned with a head of genuine human hair. This is the most valuable doll in the collection. Please do not touch."

Madame Ambassador! The words thrill me. At long last, I will be able to serve again as I was originally intended, hands extended in friendship to the people of America.

I certainly hope my visitors will pay close attention to those last, very important four words on my calling card: "Please do not touch."

※

May

Fair day finally arrived, and Aunt Eunice along with it. Dad was already off to work at Hansen's, but he'd left a note on Lois' dresser. When she opened it to read what he'd written, a quarter fell out. She picked up the coin and held it in her palm. Twenty-five cents! It felt heavy and full of promise. She read Dad's words: "For your grand adventure."

Her wish had come true! Here was exactly the right amount to ride on the rocket cars! Her hands trembled with excitement as she tied the quarter in the corner of her best hanky, the one with Amelia's *Canary* on it, so she wouldn't lose it. She double-checked the knot five times before they left the house. And she held it tight as she jounced along on the train, next to Aunt Eunice—whose head was back, mouth open in sleep—the whole way to Chicago.

Lois had the best father in the whole world. She thought about that as she fingered the knotted handkerchief. Mom used to say Lois and Dad were cut with the same cookie cutter. Full of big dreams and starry notions. He knew how much she wanted to fly across the fairgrounds in one of those double-decker rocket cars, looking down on the other fairgoers, who *would* look like cabbage worms, inching along on the ground far below. She smiled at the thought of the vast vistas she would see as she was transported through the blue Chicago sky. How was she going to stand the wait?

Nervously, she smoothed the skirt of her blue print dress. Mom had let the hem out for the third time. Even after a soaking in vinegar, the first two hemlines were still visible. Mabel had said, "It's fine. You can't hardly see anything. Besides, people are going to have their eyes on the sights at the fair, not on your dress." She'd given Lois a big hug then. "You go and have a swell time."

At this memory, the quarter grew heavier in Lois' hand. Mabel was a true-blue buddy. She'd never told anyone about what really happened to Mrs. Whitford's prize dahlias. Or why a board went missing from Mr. Stewart's fence. Only Mabel could be genuinely happy for someone else getting to go to the World's Fair.

Lois clasped the handkerchief between her hands, her feelings on a teeter-totter. Twenty-five cents would buy a nice souvenir for Mabel, who didn't have an Aunt Eunice to treat her to "educational experiences." But Dad gave her this money for *her* adventure. He would be so disappointed if she didn't use it to fulfill her dream.

The train jostled her in her seat, jolting her out of her thoughts. No sense getting into a lather. She didn't have to decide right this minute. She had the entire day ahead of her. A paper sack of cinnamon-sugar-dusted doughnuts sat in her lap. Lois ate the last one, not bothering to offer it to her dozing great-aunt. Lois studied her as she chewed. Maybe, just maybe, the Sky Ride was part of Aunt Eunice's plan. That would make it easy to decide how to spend that quarter.

She nearly jumped out of her seat when the conductor called out, "Chicago!" Aunt Eunice stirred, then gathered herself to her feet, leaning on her walking stick to step into the aisle and detrain. Wobbling like a top that had been wound too tightly, Lois followed Aunt Eunice through the station.

Aunt Eunice waved her hanky at a porter. "Please call us a cab," she said.

Lois quivered again. A cab! Wait until she told Mabel. Lois thought the cabbie was the jolliest man ever. But

Aunt Eunice frowned and clucked when he burst out singing "Life Is Just a Bowl of Cherries." Under her breath, Lois sang along:

> *"Life is just a bowl of cherries.*
> *Don't take it serious; it's too mysterious."*

They rolled down Twelfth Street, passing the Field Museum. The minute the taxi turned the last corner, the song dried right up in Lois' mouth. If Mabel had been there, they would have pinched one another to make certain they weren't dreaming. Lois had to pinch herself.

"Stay close!" Aunt Eunice steered her way through the crowds squeezing into the North Entrance. Lois followed her great-aunt through the gates and onto the fairgrounds. Stretching in front of her, as far as she could see, was a wide avenue, flanked on either side by a row of red flags. At the far end of the Avenue of Flags, the tall blue tower of the Hall of Science was topped with even more flags. To her right stood the Sears Roebuck Building, a gleaming white modern-day temple.

"Close your mouth, Lois," Aunt Eunice said. "You're letting flies in."

Lois closed her mouth but kept her eyes open wide. She'd never seen any place so shiny, so modern, so big. It was not yet nine o'clock in the morning, but neon lights blinked everywhere, reflecting off buildings painted in rich flat colors. The pamphlet she and Mabel had read and reread had described the fair as a "symphony of steel and stone and glass." It hadn't exaggerated one bit. Lois grew light-headed from trying to decide where to look.

"You, there." Aunt Eunice stopped a fair employee once they were through the entrance gate. "Could you direct us to the Food Pavilion?"

Lois had memorized the map in the pamphlet and could have led Aunt Eunice around the fairgrounds blindfolded, but listened politely while the man gave directions. They started off down the Avenue of Flags, the way he'd indicated, but then Aunt Eunice kept heading straight, instead of veering left around the end of the North Lagoon, toward Eitel's Rotisserie. Lois tugged her great-aunt's sleeve. "I think it might be this way." Her mouth watered at the smell of roasting chickens from Eitel's and the salty smell of cheese from the Dairy Building. On top of all those aromas floated the warm, sweet scent of spun sugar.

"You do, do you?" At first Aunt Eunice didn't seem inclined to listen. Then she shifted her pocketbook to her other arm and said, "Well, let's see if you're right."

Lois dawdled behind her great-aunt, bent on taking in every sight, sound, and smell. She saw a sign that brought her to a complete stop: "Sky Ride: Supreme Thrill of the Fair." Lois' head swiveled back on her neck as she turned her eyes up, up, up.

"Lois!" Aunt Eunice called back to her. "Come along. I don't want to lose you."

Lois stood transfixed as the gleaming submarine shapes of the double-decker rocket cars skimmed the steel cables far above her. She would definitely want to ride in the top deck, as high as possible!

"It looks like you were right about the route." Aunt Eunice pointed her walking stick at a building that looked to Lois like a candy-striped Pullman car. It was topped with a big sign: "The Foods and Agriculture Building." They were soon inside, each enjoying a stack of pancakes—one dime for all you could eat. And Aunt Eunice was right: a woman who looked like the Aunt Jemima in the advertisements was there. She wasn't doing much cooking, but she laughed and chatted with the fairgoers, helping to serve groaning plates of pancakes.

Lois was too excited to finish even one stack. But Aunt Eunice kept tucking in, evidently determined to get her ten cents' worth. After what seemed like a century, she sighed and then patted her mouth with a napkin. "Shall we wash up and be on our way?"

"What would you like to see first, Aunt Eunice?" Lois asked politely, when they'd finished in the washroom.

"My garden club ladies told me all the children enjoy Enchanted Island," Aunt Eunice said. "We shall begin there."

Lois held the door for her great-aunt. "Let's go out this way," she said. There was so much to see and only this one precious day in which to see it. She didn't want to waste any more time. Thank goodness she and Mabel had plotted out all kinds of ways to crisscross the fairgrounds. Lois scurried along the path between the North Lagoon and South Lagoon, past the Edison Memorial and then the Electrical Building. It was all she could do not to run ahead of her plodding great-aunt when they reached the bridge to Enchanted Island. Remembering her manners, she waited and they crossed together.

Lois felt as if she'd stepped into Storybook Land. Her attention snared by the twenty-five-foot-high cutouts of the Tin Man and the Scarecrow from the Wizard of Oz stories, Lois nearly collided with a costumed man careening around on stilts. "Lois, watch where you're going," scolded Aunt Eunice, but the man only laughed and threw confetti at them.

They tapped their toes while a troop of authentic Czechoslovakian dancers spun and twirled; shook hands with Peter Pan and his nemesis, Captain Hook—twice, once for Lois and once for Mabel—and toured inside the popular two-story model of the Radio Flyer coaster wagon. The ground-floor level was full of coaster wagons of all sizes, including teeny-tiny replicas selling for twenty-five cents. Lois thought of the quarter still knotted in her hanky. But, really, she and Mabel had outgrown wagons. So the coin stayed snug in its knot.

When it was time to move on, Aunt Eunice had her own ideas about their next destination. She dismissed both of Lois' suggestions—the Midget Village and the Prehistory Exhibit.

"It's all jimcrackery and nonsense," she said.

Lois bit her tongue, trying not to gaze too longingly at the domed building encircled by the words "The World a Million Years Ago." She'd heard that inside were replicas of saber-toothed cats and mastodons, actual size, that really moved. That would be something to see. She swallowed down her disappointment. "Well, what would you like to do next, Auntie?"

"Have a cup of tea. There." They had walked around the end of the South Lagoon, bypassing, to Lois' great relief, the Horticultural Building, the Century of Progress Club, and the Infant Incubator. They found themselves on the fringes of the Streets of Paris. Aunt Eunice pointed to an outdoor café nearby. The day was warm, and they'd already covered a lot of ground. A cool drink would hit the spot. A quick cool drink. They sat and ordered tea for Aunt Eunice and lemonade for Lois.

"Would you like to tour the Streets of Paris next?" Lois asked, fretting because Aunt Eunice had ordered hot tea. Hot tea was something her great-aunt might linger over, waiting for it to be cool enough to drink. The morning was flying by too quickly as it was.

"Certainly not!" Aunt Eunice fanned her face with her hand. "It is not appropriate for young girls. Not with that Sally Rand in there, doing that vulgar dance."

Mabel's cousin had told Mabel and Lois about Sally Rand and her famous Fan Dance.

"Naked as the day she was born under those feathered fans," he'd said.

"Have you seen her dance?" Mabel had asked. Her cousin said he tried to, but got kicked out for being underage.

"What about the Chinese Temple of Jehol?" Lois suggested. In the brochure, the temple had looked exotic and intriguing, with its brass gongs and Ming statuary.

"That's much more appropriate." Aunt Eunice stirred sugar into her tea.

Lois nearly inhaled her lemonade. Every moment they sat meant some sight went unseen.

Aunt Eunice sipped her tea as if she were a humming-bird. Talk. Sip. Talk talk. Sip.

Lois thought she might explode by the time the teacup was finally empty and the bill paid. She leaped up. "This way, Auntie." Like a dog straining at a leash, she surged ahead of her great-aunt, until Aunt Eunice's command to slow down would tug her back. Then ahead she'd go until she heard "Slow down" again.

They walked north, skirting the enormous General Exhibits Building. Up ahead loomed the twin towers of the Sky Ride. Lois' skin prickled. "I read that they're over six hundred feet high," she said, pointing upward. "Taller than any building in Chicago."

"And taller than anything needs to be," said Aunt Eunice. She ushered Lois under the formidable carved arch-way of the Chinese temple. Inside they were bombarded with color—reds and turquoises and golds—and intricate patterns everywhere, on the walls, in the rugs on the floor, even in the temple ceilings. Lois felt as if she'd tumbled into a kaleidoscope.

Aunt Eunice paused to buy a packet of postcards.

"This will be just the thing to show my sewing circle next month." She looked over at Lois. "I'm sure that quarter's burning a hole in your pocket"—Aunt Eunice smiled—"or rather in your hanky. But it shows maturity not to spend it on the first geegaw you see." Aunt Eunice nodded her approval and Lois tried not to let her mouth fly open at this unexpected compliment. "Shall we move on?"

As they left the Temple of Jehol—a bit bleary-eyed from all the decorations—Lois banged one of the big brass gongs. Mabel would have loved it, too. So Lois banged it once for her.

Outside the temple walls, they bumped into one of Aunt Eunice's acquaintances.

"Myra! How are you, my dear?" Aunt Eunice offered her cheek to the other lady and then introduced Lois.

"Quite the exposition, isn't it?" Myra placed her hand on Aunt Eunice's arm. "You'll never believe what I just rode in!"

"A gondola?" asked Aunt Eunice.

"The dragon ride?" Lois guessed.

Myra shook her head, laughed and pointed up. "The Sky Ride. Me! Can you imagine?"

Lois' admiration for the skinny old lady in front of her grew tenfold. If *she'd* gone on it, perhaps—

"Is it even safe?" Aunt Eunice pulled her pocketbook closer. "Those cables don't look sturdy enough to hold one of those contraptions they call rocket cars, let alone a dozen of them."

"Oh, but you must go!" Myra pointed to Lois. "It will give your niece here a memory she will never forget."

Aunt Eunice looked horrified. "More likely a fright she'll never forget!"

"But they're perfectly secure, Aunt Eunice!" The words slipped out before Lois could stop them. Well, in for a dime, in for a dollar. "I read that they're as safe as trolley cars. Maybe even safer."

Aunt Eunice's eyebrows were spider legs of alarm above her gray eyes. "That may be true, but nothing"— she said this with a stern glance at Myra—"will convince *me* to ride such an unhealthy distance above the ground."

Myra laughed again. "Oh, Eunice, I remember when you were always the first one up for a new experience. You were such a daredevil."

Lois stared at her great-aunt. Daredevil?

Aunt Eunice fussed with her hat. "Well, I was younger then," she said, looking quite flustered.

"Adventure is like the fountain of youth," Myra teased.

Aunt Eunice shook her head. But a smile fought to overtake her pursed lips. "You always were a caution, Myra." Aunt Eunice straightened her shoulders. "I'll see you next month at the library board meeting."

"Enjoy yourselves!" Myra called after them.

"Fountain of youth!" Aunt Eunice muttered as they walked along.

Lois' spirits fluttered around wildly, like a butterfly

caught in a net. Thanks to Myra, maybe Aunt Eunice would let her go on the Sky Ride after all. She squeezed the quarter even tighter. Maybe!

"That's the Hall of Science there, isn't it?" Aunt Eunice indicated the building with her chin. "That would certainly be educational. Shall we go?"

Lois was fascinated by The Growing Twig, an exhibit that showed, through some fancy photography, a linden growing from sapling to tree in the space of a few minutes. And she'd thought the "Chemistry of Digestion" display would be disgusting, but once she stepped inside the Robot Theater and heard the ten-foot-tall mechanical man explain certain processes of digestion while a movie of those processes played on a special screen in his shirt, she found it so interesting she stayed to listen twice. Once for her and once for Mabel. Aunt Eunice was taken with the Scholl Manufacturing Company exhibit, where she received advice about her bunions from a man in a white coat who said he had been trained under the personal supervision of Dr. William M. Scholl, noted foot authority, himself. Aunt Eunice even unlaced her oxfords for a foot massage. Lois thought they'd never get away from there.

"That was just the thing," Aunt Eunice said, retying her shoes. "I'm ready to move on again."

While her great-aunt had enjoyed the attention of the man in the white coat, Lois had been plotting how to ask about the Sky Ride. She decided that it had to seem like

Aunt Eunice's idea. "Your friend Myra was awfully nice," she began.

"Oh, speaking of friends"—Aunt Eunice pulled a piece of stationery from her pocketbook—"I nearly forgot." She scanned the letter in her hand. "Yes. That was it. My dear friend Mrs. Maxwell Wheeler wrote to tell me about an exhibit we simply must see. 'Dolls from Around the World.' Doesn't that sound nice?"

A doll exhibit definitely did not sound nice. Lois forced a smile. Perhaps they wouldn't have to stay too long.

"It isn't included in the admission price," Aunt Eunice continued. "But a portion of the ticket monies goes to support the charity projects of *Everyland Magazine*." She folded the letter back up and put it away. "Do you think we could find the Special Exhibits Hall?"

Lois knew exactly which way to go. Their route took them directly below the Sky Ride. The towers seemed like two long arms, beckoning Lois to partake of atmospheric wonders beyond imagination. As she gazed up at the tantalizing towers, into the bright sun, she found herself blinking back tears.

Aunt Eunice made a big show of handing two dimes to the thin young man at the entrance to "Dolls from Around the World." "Follow the red walkway and you won't miss a thing," he told them. "Enjoy yourselves!"

Inside the door, Aunt Eunice paused. "I've been thinking," she said. "About what Myra said. A little adventure

77

is good for the soul." She put her hand on Lois' arm. "Your father gave you that quarter to spend as you see fit. Though I choose to keep my feet firmly planted on the ground, when we are through here, you may ride on that Sky Ride."

Lois gave a little squeal, and threw her arms around her great-aunt's waist. "Oh, thank you, Aunt Eunice. Thank you!"

Aunt Eunice patted Lois briskly on the back. "Mind you, you'll have to buy your own ticket," she added.

"Of course. Yes! You've given me so much already!" Lois couldn't feel the floor under her feet. She was certain she was floating. The Sky Ride! If only Aunt Eunice had made her decision before paying the admission to the doll exhibit. Then Lois would've asked if they could head straight there. But her great-aunt would not waste the twenty cents she'd just spent. Lois crossed her fingers that it wouldn't take too long to look at the dolls.

They found the red pathway that would lead them in a spiral through the exhibit. Lois marched along, hoping to encourage Aunt Eunice to pick up her pace. But no. Her great-aunt meandered past rag dolls and stuffed animals and dolls from Germany, France, and Italy. After what seemed like hours, she pulled a fan from her pocketbook. "My lands," she said. "It's warm in here." She spied a bench. "You may finish taking the tour. I'll rest a bit. Shall we meet back here in thirty minutes?"

"Oh, we can go now if you're ready," Lois offered helpfully. Hopefully.

"No, no. I wouldn't want you to miss out on this opportunity."

"Really, I don't mind—"

Aunt Eunice dismissed Lois with her fan. "You can give me a report on what I missed."

"Okay," Lois said. Then she caught the look on Aunt Eunice's face. "I mean, yes, ma'am."

Aunt Eunice settled onto the bench with an *oof*. "Go along. Have fun."

Thirty minutes! Pure torture. How would she survive a whole half hour before her dream came true? Lois sighed, but trudged forward. If Amelia could suffer through horrible headaches every time she flew, Lois could manage a thirty-minute wait to ride in a rocket car.

She made a halfhearted effort to look at the dolls she passed, but she did stop in front of a Victorian dollhouse, furnished with the most amazing miniatures. There was even an egg no bigger than a candy sprinkle frying in a teeny skillet on a midget cookstove. Mabel would have gone crackers over the dollhouse. She was crazy about such things. That was why her father always brought her miniatures from his business trips: a tiny iron when he traveled to Pittsburgh. An orange tree no bigger than a thimble from Florida. A fairy-sized carved horse from New York. Her whole collection fit in a Lipton tea tin.

Lois noticed a sign near the dollhouse: "Take Home Replicas. Visit Our Gift Shop!"

She turned away quickly, following the path down another hall, completely lost in thought. She passed dolls made of paper and papier-mâché. The more she walked, the more she was certain that Mabel would want her to use the quarter for the Sky Ride. Think of the thrilling stories she could tell her! They would last longer than any silly souvenir. That was definitely the thing to do.

Her step and heart lighter, Lois found herself in the innermost room of the warrenlike exhibition hall. The other rooms had been chockablock with dolls of every sort and type. But this final, small chamber held only one doll. And Lois was its only visitor. She stepped closer to read the placard next to the doll. "Miss Kanagawa." All the way from Japan! Jeepers! This Miss Kanagawa doll was one of the prettiest in the exhibit. Its silky hair was the color of the strands of jet Aunt Eunice wore around her neck.

Miss Kanagawa had fifty-seven sisters, according to the placard, all of them "Ambassador Dolls" sent in hopes of improving Japanese and U.S. relations. Lois wondered how they could do that when they couldn't even talk, except maybe to say "Mama."

※

Oh, the impertinent little imp. *One* of the prettiest dolls, she thinks! And questioning my ability to be an ambassador, to boot.

But I must remember that she is only a child, after all. Lacking my wisdom. My understanding of the world. She does not yet realize the importance of helping others, as I do.

Even if the others are ill-mannered and poorly dressed.

Around the doll's feet on the display stand were mar-
velous miniatures—a small teapot, a dainty parasol, a
folded screen painted with a mountain scene. Mabel
would've loved these. Lois stepped closer to get a better
look. From here, she could see that Miss Kanagawa's eyes
were dark, like hers, but shaped like the almonds Mom
ground to make her special tea cookies. When she used to
make them, that is.

The eyes looked so real, Lois had the sense that the
doll was looking back at her. Lois blinked. Twice. But that
feeling was still there.

"You're giving me the willies," she said. Even when she
used to play with dolls, way back when, she never actually
talked to them. There was a clock on the wall behind the
doll's case. "It's been twenty minutes," Lois said. "That
should be enough time to spend with these dumb old dolls."

As soon as the words left her lips, she felt a pain. She
rubbed at it. Maybe the lemonade had been too sour. But
the discomfort wasn't in her stomach. It was higher up,
behind her sternum, and it felt like someone was poking
her with something—like that doll's parasol or something.
Whatever it was, it didn't feel good.

***

I don't understand why so many of these American children
gnaw their fingernails like mice gnaw rice kernels. It is most
perplexing. And most unbecoming. I could overlook that, I

81

suppose. And her shabby dress. But her manners! I simply can't abide it when someone thinks herself better than others. "Dumb old dolls" indeed. Does she think we are less important because we are not human? Master Tatsuhiko himself created me. Humph. I have half a mind to let her carry out her selfish decision.

But how much more satisfying it will be if this "dumb" doll teaches this child a lesson!

All in the name of friendship and goodwill, of course.

✳

Lois leaned her head against the doll's display case. Once, when she had nearly fainted at Cousin Catherine's wedding, Mom had told her to take long, even, deep breaths. Maybe that would help now. She tried.

It didn't.

She looked up and found herself eye to eye with the doll. It was as if those eyes were movie screens, shimmering with images that slowly flickered into focus. Lois couldn't tear her gaze away.

She was looking back at the first day of grade school. She'd forgotten her lunch. And there was Mabel saying, "I've got egg salad. Would you like half?" The scene shifted forward in time to show Mabel, cross-legged, doing some kind of hand sewing. She was making a sash, for Lois, who'd been voted Queen of the May for the third-grade pageant. Mabel stitched on felt letters that spelled out "Queen Lois." The scene changed again and now Lois saw her as she was a few days ago, flopped on her stomach on the bed, poring over the fair pamphlet. She heard Mabel say, "Now, it looks like if you go left instead of right at the end of the Avenue of Flags, you'll be closer to the entrance to the Social Science Hall."

Lois rubbed her eyes. What was happening? She shook herself, hard, to clear her head. Her handkerchief flew out of her hand and landed with a soft *whup* on the floor. She bent to pick it up.

❋

A good friend gives our heart wings.

❋

Lois stood up so fast her head was spinning like an airplane propeller. "Who's there?" she asked, peering into the dark edges of the room.

No one answered.

Time to get out of there. Back to Aunt Eunice. Some fresh air would do them both good. They'd been in this place long enough. She'd done what Aunt Eunice had wanted all day. It was her turn now. The Sky Ride was calling her. Lois reached again for the hanky, still on the floor. "Ouch!" Another poke in the chest. This one was hard enough to make her need to sit down. She pulled her knees in, wrapping her dress around her legs.

One more scene rolled like a player piano scroll through Lois' mind: Mabel, this morning, come to send Lois off. Her elbows poked through her thin sweater, and she was barefoot to save wear and tear on her shoes.

She'd gotten up early to make cinnamon doughnuts for Lois' train ride.

Lois looked over at the doll. It stood there, the same hint of a smile on its red lips. Its arms still rested gracefully at its sides. It didn't appear to have moved at all. Of course, it couldn't move at all. It was only a doll. And yet something had happened here in this room.

"I guess you aren't so dumb after all," Lois said.

The doll said nothing—of course—but its eyes gazed knowingly at her.

Lois rested her chin on her knees, looking back at Miss Kanagawa. Ambassador of Friendship.

Friendship.

Lois chewed on a fingernail. Then another. That ride would last, what, five minutes? A good friend would last a lifetime.

With a long exhale, Lois reached for the handkerchief, still on the floor, and picked it up. The flash of yellow was a vibrant reminder of her dreams.

Canary yellow. Amelia's *Canary*. Amelia, who worked at odd jobs to earn enough money for flying lessons, holding on to her dream all the while.

Lois hefted the cloth-wrapped coin. Slowly, carefully, she picked at the fabric to untie the knot. Soon the quarter rested in her palm.

She set it, warm and solid, on the floor. Then she ran her hands over the *Canary* printed on each corner of the handkerchief. A smile flitted across her lips. She thought Amelia would approve.

Lois folded her precious souvenir handkerchief into fourths and tucked it into the doll's obi as a small token of thanks.

It was after midnight when she and Aunt Eunice arrived home, tired, bedraggled but elated, from the fair. Mabel's bedroom light was still on, so Lois ran right over. The smile on Mabel's face when she opened that carved wooden apple to find the miniature tea set tucked inside gave Lois' heart such wings that it soared—at least six hundred feet high.

❉

MISS KANAGAWA

It is a blessing that none of my sisters can see me now, with this wrinkled handkerchief in my obi. What would they think? It is distressing to appear so; most unbecoming for an ambassador.

And yet it is my duty to be accepting of these odd American customs. She is a child, after all. I am sure she meant well, even if her token of appreciation has marred my appearance. And by the lightness of her step I surmise she has made a wise decision. With no small help from me, of course. I think I am beginning to understand Master Tatsuhiko's teaching that good and bad can be intertwined with one another.

Oh dear. That peculiar feeling is back again. Above the spot where that handkerchief rests, on my left side. Humph.

It is not painful, as it was before. In fact, the sensation puts me in mind of a taiko drummer, striking the drumheads with the bachi sticks in a peaceful rhythm. Yes, if I think of it as a drumbeat, the feeling is not so bad. Not so bad at all.

85

September 1937

Curtain Brothers Auctions
Kansas City, Missouri

I N V O I C E

Date: September 6, 1937

Sold to: Mrs. Arthur Weldon
Clearbrook, Kentucky

Items sold:
One fossil (megalodon tooth)
Specimen-quality shell, junonia, orig. Sanibel Island,
    Florida
Maury's Manual of Geography, by M. F. Maury, LL.D,
    published 1870, (University Publishing Company)
Japanese-style doll (Yoshitoku Doll Company)

Total Due: $250.00
PAID IN FULL

MISS KANAGAWA

After a long slumber, I feel daylight on my face again. When I was removed from my trunk, I sought out Brigitte. But the Bleuette doll was nowhere to be found. After a moment of gathering my bearings, I realized I didn't sense any other dolls around me.

Instead, I was surrounded by what looked to be the debris left after a high tide: piles of shells in assorted sizes, from no bigger than a child's fingernail to those that could barely be contained in a grown man's two hands; mottled beach stones, some as rough as a stormy sea and some as smooth as the glass in a Japanese fisherman's float. There were shelves filled with things I had no names for. And in every slice of space not occupied by any of these items, there were books. And books and books! An endless number of them, stacked and shelved and stacked some more.

I surmise that someone will be returning to this room; I do hope it's someone interesting. Otherwise, my time here will be deadly dull. Because, though I am skilled in many ways, I cannot read. No doll can. Well, Miss Japan once told the story of a doll who, when fully awakened, found she could read. But Miss Japan was one to chatter like the wagtail perched in a cherry tree in spring. Such a story surely falls in the category of those about flying dragons and empresses whose kites carry them over palace walls.

So here I am with nothing but beach flotsam and paper bricks for company. Compared to these, the Madame Alexander dolls were charming social companions. I cannot understand how I will resume my duties as an ambassador in this place. But any samurai knows that life is a balance between understanding and mystery.

Until the way is revealed to me, I will be patient and steadfast.

For as long as is needed.

✳

Willie Mae Marcum

"No sense sticking your nose out the front door every five minutes. Miz Junkins ain't coming." Ma switched baby Franklin to the other breast, burping him quick in between, before he started caterwauling loud as the wind outside. "Not in weather like this. Raining pigs and chickens the way it is."

"Come help me with the wash," Marvel said to Willie Mae. "You could scrub awhile."

Willie Mae's conscience tugged her away from the door. Marvel was getting over the grippe, her face still as white as the paste Miz Junkins used to patch up the worn-out books she brought. And Ma was surely right. November had slipped in all icy-like, and the trail down Cut Shin Creek was steep as a mule's face. Miz Junkins' horse,

89

Maisie, was as sure-footed as they come, but it wouldn't be sensible to take chances. If she got hurt, she'd lose her government WPA job, and then who would take care of those three little ones of hers? Not Mr. Junkins. He'd left a note on the kitchen table that he was headed to California for work but had sent no word—nor money—these past six months.

Willie Mae took her big sister's place at the basin. The lye soap stung her chapped hands as she pushed Franklin's diapers down and up, down and up, over the crenulated surface of the tin washboard. All she could think as she scrubbed was that babies were work, pure and simple, and that was why she planned never to birth any.

"Suits me fine anyways. Her not coming," Ma said. She had finished nursing Franklin. Her pats on his back produced a prodigious burp. "Every two weeks that library woman shows up and then I gotta spend the next fourteen days prying that speckled nose of yours out of some foolish book." Ma rocked Franklin all herky-jerky in the hickory rocker. "You be a good boy, Franklin, and fall right to sleep. I got piecing to do."

"Here, Ma. I'll cozy him." Marvel took the baby as well as Ma's place on the rocker seat. Ma situated herself closer to the kerosene lamp, where her quilt lay wrapped in a frayed white sheet to keep it clean. Since Mr. Pritchard over to Wisdom told her he'd pay twelve dollars for any quilt she made, Ma had turned into a whirling dervish of a quilter.

That white sheet put Willie Mae to mind of Mary

Rose. Ma had worn a groove in the floor, rocking *that* child when she was a baby, all the while singing hymns and such in that cherry-sweet voice of hers. That was before the mine accident where Pap's back got all stove-in and his insides were hurt so bad. It wasn't two weeks after Pap's funeral that Mary Rose got the fever and passed over herself. Ma didn't sing anymore, not even the smallest lullaby to baby Franklin.

"You need something to read, Willie Mae, you could read Theodore's letter again." Marvel's mind wasn't as quick as some her age, but her heart was bigger than the entire state of Kentucky. She knew how much Willie Mae loved to read, loved words, and encouraged her every which way. Ma frowned but didn't say anything on account of it being Marvel doing the suggesting. "It's still there, in the sugar bowl."

This was a safe spot for Theodore's letters, now that sugar was on the list of the many groceries the family couldn't buy. It was a good thing Theo sent them stamps from time to time or they'd never be able to write him back.

Willie Mae wrung out the last diaper and pegged it to the line strung across the room. What with the steam from the wash water and the damp from the diapers and the cold wriggling its way around the rags stuffed in the broken windowpanes, the room felt clammy as a grave. Willie Mae dried her hands and tugged her sweater tighter. Three years ago, when she was a chubby eight-year-old, she could barely button it around her. After the last few years of slim pickins at the table, the sweater hung on her like she was wearing one of Theodore's. She fetched the letter and began to read it aloud: "My dearest family—"

"That's about my favorite part," Marvel interrupted. "We are dear to Theo, ain't we?" Shivering, she wrapped a corner of the quilt Ma was piecing around her bony shoulders.

Ma looked up from the squares of blue shirting. "If that boy says something, it is so," she said. She sighed before bending over her work once more. "He's as honest as the day is long."

"My dearest family," Willie Mae read again. It was a comfort to her, too, to see those words on the page, and to taste them in her mouth. Reading them twice was as sweet as getting a whole peppermint stick all to herself.

I think you would find me quite handsome in my new beard. I'm so good-looking that folks keep mistaking me for that movie star Basil Rathbone.

Marvel laughed. "Think of it—our Theo a movie star." Ma harrumphed and bit off a length of thread. She handed the needle to Marvel, who quickly threaded it. Ma's eyes had weakened so, she couldn't see to do that herself anymore.

Some of the fellows here have spent more time in an office than out of doors and so whimper like kicked dogs at the end of the workday. Me, I suck up all the fresh air here in Oregon that I can. Fresh air was in short supply in the mines. The work I do ain't all that much different—I'm still swinging a pickax—but it's where I'm doing it that makes all the difference. If you precious ones was here with me, I'd say I'd found heaven on earth. But a CCC camp's no place for women. Our new barracks are so small there ain't room enough to cuss a cat without getting a mouthful of fur. But we manage.

Willie Mae was thankful for Theo's CCC job. The Civilian Conservation Corps—even the name sounded important. She did wish President Roosevelt hadn't sent him so far off. Seemed to her there were trails could be built and trees planted in Kentucky, same as in Oregon. Theo said his six months away would slip by, but to Willie Mae even one day without her big brother was too long. She couldn't wait until his time was up and he'd come home.

Last night, this ol' Tennessee boy commenced to playing on his guitar, and the next thing I knew, a bunch of us was singing 'Pretty Polly,' and 'It Rained a Mist' and 'Old Smokey.' It made me feel like I was back home, all of us singing together like we used to.

Your loving son and brother,
Theodore Wilson Marcum

93

The twenty-five-dollar allotment check that had come with the letter was already spent. Thanks to it, there was a ham shank simmering in the pot with the soup beans.

"I bet Theo sings circles round those other boys," said Marvel.

"I bet he does," agreed Willie Mae.

Ma didn't say anything and Willie Mae couldn't read her face. For a long time now, Ma had been a mystery, not giving one clue as to what was going on in her thoughts.

Willie Mae folded up the letter and put it back in the sugar bowl. The house grew so quiet, the only thing she could hear was the baby snuffling in his sleep and the hiss of the kerosene lamp. "Shall I start some corn bread?"

"That'd be a help." Ma didn't look up from her stitching. "The wood box need filling?"

Willie Mae peeked at the box beside the stove. Marvel had taken over the job of keeping it filled since Theo had gone away, but seeing as she was still puny from the grippe, Willie Mae would take a turn. She pulled a shabby coat from a peg by the front door. "Back in two shakes of a lamb's tail."

Ma nodded absently. Marvel's head bobbed as she rocked the baby, asleep now herself, by the looks of it.

Willie Mae jumped over the puddle at the bottom of the steps and allowed herself one longing look down the road. She wished so hard to see Miz Junkins and Maisie coming along that she conjured up their images. Then she looked again—this was no daydream. It was real.

"Miz Junkins!" Willie Mae waved her arm till it like to fall off.

When horse and rider drew near enough for conversation, Miz Junkins said, "I couldn't disappoint my best customer." She slid off Maisie's back, threw her reins over the front porch rail, and undid her saddlebags.

Dripping, Willie Mae clomped back up the steps and pulled open the front door. "Ma! Look who's here!"

Ma's brow wrinkled, but she set her quilt aside. "Marvel, you get on up and let Miz Junkins have a seat. Willie Mae, see if there's coffee left in that pot."

"Don't stop stitching on my account, Laralee." Miz Junkins set down her saddlebags to take the cup of hot coffee from Willie Mae and swallow a grateful sip. "And, Marvel, you stay put."

"Sit here, Miz Junkins." Willie Mae pulled over the stool Pap had made. Though she was dying to see what treasures those saddlebags held this visit, she minded her manners.

Ma took Miz Junkins' patched wool coat and hung it over the open oven door. "We need to get you dried out and warmed up. Willie Mae, go fetch the rail fence quilt."

Willie Mae ran to the bed she and Marvel shared, snatched off the quilt, and hurried back. She handed it to Miz Junkins, who wrapped it around her shoulders. Willie Mae plopped down at her feet.

"I finished this." Willie Mae handed back *The Windy Hill*, the book she'd checked out two weeks earlier.

Miz Junkins took another sip of coffee, then set the graniteware cup on the table to take the book. "How did you like it?" She tucked it back in one of her saddlebags.

"I liked it fine."

"That answer's as thin as stone soup." The librarian smiled. "The truth won't hurt my feelings."

Willie Mae hated to appear ungrateful when Miz Junkins traveled so far to bring books she thought Willie Mae would enjoy. But maybe they were good enough friends now to tell it straight. "I suppose some *would* like to read about living in fine houses with butlers and rich uncles, but that isn't my fancy. I long to read about someone like me and my kin."

"Well, Miss Willie Mae Marcum, that sounds like a mighty fine idea." Miz Junkins smiled again. "Maybe *you* will have to write that book someday."

"Sarah, do not put any more foolishness in that girl's head." Ma bit off another hank of thread. "It's bad enough she reads them books. Heaven help us if she gets her mind stuck on writing them, too."

Willie Mae ducked her head so Ma wouldn't see her face. Because if she saw it, she might see that it was too late to stop the foolishness. Willie Mae dursn't let herself think on it, but every story she read made two or three sprout up in her own head. She wrote them down on any spare scrap of paper she could find—the envelopes Theo's letters came in, labels steamed off the lard pails, even the insides of saltine boxes—and hid them in an empty sugar sack under her mattress.

Miz Junkins finished her coffee. "I brought you *A Little Princess* today—but next time, I'll see if I can round up a copy of *The Adventures of Tom Sawyer*. That might sit better with you." She rummaged in her saddlebags. "Oh, and I brought a *Ladies' Home Journal* for you, Marvel. Not even a year old!" She buckled up her bag. "I best be on my way. Thank you for the coffee and the quilt. I do believe the warmth will stick with me clear till I ride into my own yard."

Willie Mae went out on the porch and watched while Miz Junkins buckled the saddlebags back on, untied Maisie's reins, and pulled herself into the saddle. Since it was bad luck to watch a friend go out of sight, she turned back inside as soon as horse and rider were on their way.

After supper and chores were finished, Ma allowed Willie Mae to burn the kerosene lamp for ten precious minutes so she could commence reading the book Miz Junkins had brought. Willie Mae offered to read it aloud, but Ma said no thank you. "Seeing as both Marvel and Franklin are asleep," she added. Willie Mae accepted Ma's answer but wished she could understand why her mother had such a strong notion against reading and books.

Willie Mae was disappointed to find that *A Little Princess*—about a girl whose name was Sara Crewe—had a rich and loving father in India who sent her to a boarding school in London with orders to the headmistress to give Sara anything she wanted. It was all Willie Mae could do to keep from grinding her teeth at yet another story about a girl whose life was different as different could be from hers.

"Time's up," Ma called softly. "That a good one?" she asked.

"It reads right along," said Willie Mae, avoiding a direct answer. She didn't want to do or say anything that might make Ma tell Miz Junkins to stop riding down Cut Shin Creek to see them. Because, truth to tell, even a book she didn't like was better than no book at all.

When she came two weeks later, Miz Junkins looked about to burst with news. "I couldn't get a copy of *Tom Sawyer* for you this time," she said to Willie Mae. "But I believe you will forgive me when you hear what I have to say. First, I need to speak with your ma."

The two women spoke in low tones at the far corner of the cabin. Willie Mae could not imagine what they were talking about. Nothing to do but wait. She went over in her mind the report she was going to give Miz Junkins about *A Little Princess*. The book wasn't half bad, after she got it started. That Sara girl had spunk after all, which got her through some tough spots, especially after her pap died and all the diamond mine money was lost and she had to go to work as the cook's errand girl. Willie Mae rubbed her bare legs to warm them. Course, things perked up plenty for Sara, what with the Indian Gentleman taking her in at the end of the book. But she'd had dark, cold times, too, like Willie Mae.

And speak of cold! December was knocking at the

door, carrying a heap of cold in its pack. Ma kept putting aside pennies each month from Theo's check to get the girls some wool stockings. Marvel would need them first, as she was still sickly. Ma had dosed her with boiled molasses and kerosene but to no avail. Marvel couldn't shake feeling puny. Willie Mae shivered.

"Willie Mae." Ma shifted Franklin to her other hip. "Miz Junkins has something to say to you."

"Ask you, really." Miz Junkins' eyes twinkled like she was Santy Claus hisself. "What would you say to a job?"

"A job?" This was the last thing Willie Mae expected.

"Mrs. Trent is looking for someone to read to her mother, keep her company. The lady who's been doing it is needed at home to take care of her sister's new baby. She can start up again in January. But till then, they need somebody." Miz Junkins clasped her hands together. "They will pay you five dollars a week and room and board, Willie Mae! To read! And maybe a few light chores." Her grin stretched nearly ear to ear.

"Who will help around here?" Willie Mae looked at Ma. "Marvel's on the mend yet."

Ma jiggled Franklin, who was rubbing his eyes and fussing. "She's still a big help. We can manage."

Five dollars a week. To keep someone company. To read aloud! The Trents lived in the finest house in the big town of Clearbrook and owned half of Lincoln County, to boot. Willie Mae guessed they would have more books than all of the traveling libraries put together. "If you're sure you'll be fine . . ."

Ma nodded. "It's a Christmas gift, Willie Mae. A pure gift."

Willie Mae glanced at the calendar Ma had tacked by the stove. It'd be four full weeks until January 1. Four weeks. She quickly did the sum in her head. Twenty dollars! That would buy wool stockings and then some. Maybe even real doctoring for Marvel. "I'll do it."

Miz Junkins waited while Willie Mae gathered up her few things in a feed sack. Careful not to let anyone see, Willie Mae slid her secret writings out from underneath the mattress. She felt a bit wobbly as she said good-bye to Marvel, and Franklin, and Ma. A few pesky tears even tried to push their way out of her eyes. She'd never been gone from home even one night, let alone one month. She swallowed hard. Could she do it? She thought of Sara Crewe, being sent off to that boarding school in London, far from her beloved papa. Time to put some steel in her spine. She kissed Ma's cheek. "I'll see you in a month," she said, with as much cheer as she could muster.

"Mind your manners," Ma said. "And don't sweep after the sun goes down."

"Don't you think I know better than that?" Her mother's advice made Willie Mae smile. Any fool knew that was a sure way to lure bad luck. "I won't look in any mirrors at midnight, t'either."

Outside, Miz Junkins mounted Maisie, then tugged Willie Mae up behind her. Maisie snorted once or twice to make her opinion about the situation known, but she plodded along regular. "She knows the way to town blindfolded," said Miz Junkins. "She'll have us there in a few hours."

Willie Mae shivered in her threadbare coat. Miz Junkins reached into her own coat pocket and pulled out a thin wool scarf. "Tie this over your head," she told Willie Mae. "Helps to keep your head covered."

Willie Mae obeyed. The scarf helped—and so did clinging to Miz Junkins, to share her warmth. Willie Mae got so comfy perched on Maisie's back that she might have been sawing logs if she hadn't been preoccupied with memorizing every inch of the ride so she could tell Marvel and Ma about it later. And write about it to Theo, too. They rode under the twisted arms of coffee trees, pods clicking as the wind swept through the branches. Willie Mae reached out to run her fingers across the scaly black bark of a bare persimmon tree, and she scootched closer to Miz Junkins when they passed a stand of chinkapin oaks, white trunks glowing ghostly.

After they'd been riding for some time, they came upon a glossy green holly tree, bursting with red berries. Miz Junkins stopped Maisie, slid off, and drew a knife from her saddlebag. She cut several large sprigs. "Won't this make my house festive for Christmas?" she said.

"They're good luck, too," Willie Mae added, gingerly holding the clippings while the librarian remounted. Miz Junkins then took her treasures and balanced them in her arms the rest of the ride.

Willie Mae knew Miz Junkins had to be bone tired from all her riding and carrying. She didn't mind that they weren't talking. It gave her mind time to spin stories. She was particularly fond of the one she was growing in her head about a possum that ate too many persimmons. She had done that once herself when she was younger and paid the price with many hurried trips to the necessary that night. Pap had laughed at her predicament. "Greed has a bitter reward," he said. But he also plucked a few green persimmons and boiled them up to make her a tea that calmed her insides down considerable.

She was so tangled up in the tale she was weaving that she nearly missed the Clearbrook city limits sign. She shivered again, but not from the cold this time. "Do you think I'll do?" she asked, her voice as thin as her coat.

"I wouldn't have suggested you otherwise." Miz Junkins eased Maisie to a stop in the road in front of a grand white house. "Here we be."

Willie Mae slid off, her legs wobbly as licorice whips. She reached up for her feed sack. "Thank you for the ride, Miz Junkins."

"I'll walk you to the door." Miz Junkins slid off Maisie's back, handing Willie Mae a sprig of holly. "For luck," she said. "Now come along." She headed briskly for the house, across the sprawling lawn. Willie Mae hightailed it right behind her, feed sack in one hand and holly in the other. She wondered if they would go to that massive front door, black and glossy like Ma's fresh-washed hair.

Halfway into the yard, Miz Junkins turned. They'd be knocking at the back door, it appeared.

Miz Junkins stopped at the stoop. "Go ahead," she said, indicating that Willie Mae should knock.

Willie Mae summoned her courage and rapped at the door. A lady in a print apron soon appeared.

"Miz Trent?" Willie Mae asked.

The lady laughed. "Not me. But you must be that child from the holler. Thanks for bringing her, Miz Junkins. You-all had best come in out of the cold." The door creaked open wider to allow them passage. Willie Mae took a small step into the warmth. One breath and she was practically slobbering like an old hound dog. This was heaven: all these good smells in one place. She sniffed again.

"I need to get home to my children," said Miz Junkins, who had remained on the stoop. "I'll check on you from time to time." She scooped Willie Mae into a hug.

Willie Mae nodded. "I'd like that."

Miz Junkins and the apron lady said their good-byes and the door shut. Willie Mae felt smaller than ever in that big, shiny kitchen.

"You hungry?" the apron lady asked.

Willie Mae put on her best company manners. "No, ma'am."

The lady got a sad look on her face. "You mean I cooked you up a nice supper and you ain't even going to taste it?" She clucked her tongue.

"I didn't mean to be rude, ma'am." Willie Mae licked her lips. "I could manage a bite, I suppose."

"That's a relief." The lady held out her hands for Willie

Mae's coat. "Here, I'll take that. You go on and sit over there."

The kitchen table was set with a covered dish. Willie Mae sat down and a full glass of milk appeared to the right of the plate. The lady in the apron lifted the cover and Willie Mae could not believe her eyes. Greens, mashed potatoes, and a whole pork chop! And there was a roll, and jam.

"Go ahead. Eat." The lady laid a napkin in Willie Mae's lap. "You're going to need your strength."

For the next twenty minutes or so, the only sounds in the kitchen were the ticking of the clock, Willie Mae's chewing, and the apron lady chuckling here and there.

Willie Mae ate every bite of food on the plate, eating till her stomach felt like it might burst. She wished she could save some of this feast to share with Marvel and Ma. Thinking of them eating cushaw squash and soup beans made her feel bad. But with her gone, they'd each get a bigger share of the vittles. And when she went back, think of the groceries she could take with her! Maybe she could afford a whole ham.

The kitchen door swung open. "Olive?" a woman's voice called out.

"Yes, ma'am." The apron lady—Olive—hopped up.

A woman with curly white hair and a dress the color of a pawpaw flower stepped into the kitchen. "Has the girl—?" She stopped when she saw Willie Mae. "I see the answer to my question is right here, at the table."

Willie Mae dropped her fork and took a run at her

face with her napkin. She stood up to introduce herself proper. "I'm Willie Mae Marcum, ma'am."

The lady smiled, waving Willie Mae to sit back down. "Don't stop eating on my account." She fiddled with the gold necklace resting on her large bosom. "Lord knows, you'll need your strength for Mother." She paced around the kitchen, lifted the lid of one of the pots on the stove, and peeked in. "Oh, that smells wonderful, Olive. Not too much paprika?"

Olive shook her head. "Not even a dash. I know Mrs. Weldon has a touchy stomach."

"Yes. Well." Mrs. Trent lifted one eyebrow and let the lid drop back on the pot. "Send the girl—what's your name again?"

"Willie Mae."

"Send Willie Mae out to me when she's finished eating. Make sure her hands are clean. And see if there's a comb you can run through her hair." She turned and left the kitchen.

"I'm finished. Thank you." Willie Mae picked up her plate. "Where shall I wash this up?"

"Don't mind the dish." Olive took it from her. "You are going to have your hands full enough with Mrs. Weldon. Come on, then. Let's get you cleaned up and presentable."

Her fingernails and neck and ears scrubbed pink and her hair parted and plaited and tied with two blue bows, Willie Mae was led to the parlor where Mrs. Trent sat knitting. "Well, don't you look sweet."

Willie Mae listened for a hint of phony in her words but heard none. Maybe she really did look sweet. Imagine! Wait till she told Theo!

"Let me show you your room." Mrs. Trent set her knitting aside and stood. She led the way out of the parlor and up a wide set of stairs with two landings. At the far end of the second landing was a closed door. "That's my mother's room," she said, pausing briefly. They climbed another, narrower flight of stairs.

"I hope you'll be comfortable." Mrs. Trent opened the door.

"It looks like a picture in the Monkey Ward catalog," Willie Mae blurted out.

Mrs. Trent laughed. "Well, it's hardly that fancy."

It might not have been fancy to someone like Mrs. Trent, but to Willie Mae, this room was a Cinderella surprise. A tidy bed, covered in a chenille bedspread of blue and pink roses, was tucked snug under the dormer. Willie Mae moved to it, running her fingers over the bumpy chenille. She imagined herself lying there—a whole bed all to herself!—and looking through those sheer white curtains to the sky outside.

Mrs. Trent pointed around the room. "There's a desk there, and feel free to use all the drawers in that dresser."

All of Willie Mae's possessions would easily fit in one of the drawers. Imagine owning so many clothes that you needed a whole dresser.

"The bathroom is down the hall, that way." Mrs. Trent smoothed a tiny wrinkle from the bedspread.

No running to the privy on a dark, cold morning! Willie Mae could scarcely take in such luxury.

Olive had followed them up the stairs. "I sleep on this floor, too," she said. "If you need anything in the night, have a bad dream—anything—you call out and I'll be right in."

Willie Mae nodded her thanks.

A clock chimed somewhere in the hall. "Seven o'clock already?" Mrs. Trent fiddled with her necklace again. "It's time to meet Mother. Come, child." She led the way down the stairs and across the landing to that closed door.

Mrs. Trent hesitated a moment, then knocked.

"Come in." The voice sounded pleasant enough to Willie Mae's ears. She followed Mrs. Trent inside the room.

"Oh!" She couldn't contain herself as she took it all in. There wasn't a place her eyes could light that didn't hold something to take her breath away. Look at that seashell the size of Ma's teakettle! Willie Mae bet a person could hear the ocean in such a shell. And shelf after shelf was lined with baskets and bowls and bins, overflowing with rocks that put her to mind of planets and dinosaurs and mysteries.

"Close your mouth, child."

The words caught Willie Mae up short and she clamped her lips together.

"You can talk, can't you?" Now Willie Mae saw the speaker, an old lady who looked like one of those apple-core dolls, all wrinkled of face; a mane of white duck down flared out above her forehead and behind her ears.

"Yes, ma'am." Willie Mae didn't know if she should curtsy. She ducked her head. "My name is Willie Mae Marcum."

The lady stuck her neck out like a banty rooster. "A holler girl? And you can read?" It was a question that implied the answer must be no.

"Yes, ma'am. Miz Junkins says I'm one of her best readers." Willie Mae scratched behind her left pigtail.

"Melba, she doesn't have fleas, does she?"

Mrs. Trent sighed so quietly that only Willie Mae could hear. "She comes from a good family, Mother. No fleas."

"Doesn't look like she eats regular." The apple-seed eyes squinched up. "She won't get sickly on me, will she?"

Willie Mae didn't wait for Mrs. Trent to answer. "I'm healthy as a horse, ma'am. Even when Marvel and Ma got the grippe, it skipped me clean over."

"This won't do at all." The apple core lady tugged at the shawl draped over her shoulders. "She's probably a carrier."

"Mother, don't be ridiculous." Mrs. Trent nudged Willie Mae forward. "What would you like her to read to you this evening?"

Now it was Mrs. Weldon's turn to sigh, only it wasn't quiet. In fact, it was so loud Willie Mae couldn't imagine it really came from that frail body. "I suppose she'll make an utter mess of *The Adventures of Tom Sawyer*," she finally said.

Willie Mae scanned the rows of books behind the old

Miz Junkins stopped at the stoop. "Go ahead," she said, indicating that Willie Mae should knock.

Willie Mae summoned her courage and rapped at the door. A lady in a print apron soon appeared.

"Miz Trent?" Willie Mae asked.

The lady laughed. "Not me. But you must be that child from the holler. Thanks for bringing her, Miz Junkins. You-all had best come in out of the cold." The door creaked open wider to allow them passage. Willie Mae took a small step into the warmth. One breath and she was practically slobbering like an old hound dog. This was heaven: all these good smells in one place. She sniffed again.

"I need to get home to my children," said Miz Junkins, who had remained on the stoop. "I'll check on you from time to time." She scooped Willie Mae into a hug.

Willie Mae nodded. "I'd like that."

Miz Junkins and the apron lady said their good-byes and the door shut. Willie Mae felt smaller than ever in that big, shiny kitchen.

"You hungry?" the apron lady asked.

Willie Mae put on her best company manners. "No, ma'am."

The lady got a sad look on her face. "You mean I cooked you up a nice supper and you ain't even going to taste it?" She clucked her tongue.

"I didn't mean to be rude, ma'am." Willie Mae licked her lips. "I could manage a bite, I suppose."

"That's a relief." The lady held out her hands for Willie

Mae's coat. "Here, I'll take that. You go on and sit over there."

The kitchen table was set with a covered dish. Willie Mae sat down and a full glass of milk appeared to the right of the plate. The lady in the apron lifted the cover and Willie Mae could not believe her eyes. Greens, mashed potatoes, and a whole pork chop! And there was a roll, and jam.

"Go ahead. Eat." The lady laid a napkin in Willie Mae's lap. "You're going to need your strength."

For the next twenty minutes or so, the only sounds in the kitchen were the ticking of the clock, Willie Mae's chewing, and the apron lady chuckling here and there.

Willie Mae ate every bite of food on the plate, eating till her stomach felt like it might burst. She wished she could save some of this feast to share with Marvel and Ma. Thinking of them eating cushaw squash and soup beans made her feel bad. But with her gone, they'd each get a bigger share of the vittles. And when she went back, think of the groceries she could take with her! Maybe she could afford a whole ham.

The kitchen door swung open. "Olive?" a woman's voice called out.

"Yes, ma'am." The apron lady—Olive—hopped up.

A woman with curly white hair and a dress the color of a pawpaw flower stepped into the kitchen. "Has the girl—?" She stopped when she saw Willie Mae. "I see the answer to my question is right here, at the table."

Willie Mae dropped her fork and took a run at her

lady. As luck would have it, the words "Tom Sawyer" jumped right off one of the spines. She walked straight across the room, took the book, and opened it up. Her heart fluttered in her chest like a Kentucky warbler as she began to read.

> *The old lady pulled her spectacles down and looked over them about the room; then she put them up and looked out under them. She seldom or never looked through them for so small a thing as a boy. . . .*

"I'll have Olive bring your warm milk up in an hour, Mother." Mrs. Trent sidled out of the room.

"I'm going to get a fractious head if I have to strain so to listen." Mrs. Weldon patted the seat of the chair next to her. "Come closer. Sit here."

✳

Though she is scarcely dressed in silk, I sense a fellow samurai in the room. One who knows that the carrot, not the rod, makes the donkey move.

✳

Willie Mae eased across the room like she would in the presence of a skittish animal and lightly perched on the edge of the chair, all the while reading. She stumbled a few times, which triggered some thorny words from Mrs. Weldon, but they hardly counted for anything. Pap would've said this little old lady was all growl and no snap.

Willie Mae would have to pinch herself when she went to bed this night. Imagine, getting paid to read *Tom Sawyer*! Wait till she wrote Theo!

❋

Within a few days, they'd settled into a routine. Willie Mae would read to Mrs. Weldon after lunch and dinner and await her call at other times for odds and ends. When she wasn't with Mrs. Weldon, she had time to read and write on her own. Mrs. Trent had seen her scribbling the second night she was there and the very next day presented Willie Mae with one of those new coil-spring notebooks. "Let me know when this one is filled and you need another," she'd said. Willie Mae had felt exactly like Sara Crewe did when the Indian Gentleman arranged to have presents sent to her while she was living in Miss Minchin's attic. She'd written Theo all about it that very night.

During the day, when she wasn't needed by Mrs. Weldon, she also made herself helpful to Olive even though Olive said that wasn't part of her chores. But pitching in helped the time pass more quickly. Olive found out that Willie Mae had a weakness for icebox cookies, so she baked them every day. "Those squalls from up there"—Olive tossed her head toward Mrs. Weldon's second-floor realm—"have quieted considerable since you came. These cookies are small thanks for your part in that."

"All I do is read to her or listen to her," said Willie Mae. "That's nothing."

"It's something to us," said Olive. "I swan—Mrs.

Trent's been so lighthearted she could put the star atop the town Christmas tree without a ladder."

On the fifth day, Mrs. Weldon rang for Willie Mae before she'd finished her oatmeal. Willie Mae cleaned up real quick and flew up the stairs, two at a time.

"You sound like a horse, panting so," Mrs. Weldon grumbled. She sat behind a long desk, nearly hidden by piles of stones. "This isn't a racetrack. But perhaps coming from the hills you wouldn't know how to behave in a proper home."

Hot words boiled in Willie Mae's mouth, but she swallowed them down. Pap always said you could catch more flies with honey than vinegar, but it appeared Mrs. Weldon didn't know that. Willie Mae stood, forcing herself to breathe as quietly as possible to cool off. When she felt she could speak in a normal voice again, she asked, "Was there something you needed my help with, ma'am?"

Mrs. Weldon's wrinkled lips pursed so tight they looked like some kind of creature all to themselves. It took powerful control for Willie Mae not to out-and-out stare.

Mrs. Weldon's hand rested on a large gray rock with white streaks folded through it. "I have decided it is time to organize my rock collection." She smacked her lips in dismay. "I suppose it'd be hopeless to try to teach you how to categorize them."

Willie Mae moved closer to the table. She picked up two stones on the edge of the desk, nearest her. "These look like the same sort of rock. What are they called?"

"Lucky guess." Mrs. Weldon sniffed. "They are the same type. Sedimentary. Formed when stones are cemented together by mud and such."

Willie Mae reached for another rock. "Is this sedimentary, too?"

"Yes, yes." Mrs. Weldon waved her hand impatiently. "Put them in that box there."

Willie Mae did as she was told, and then she picked up a small stone that put her to mind of a speckled bird's egg. "This one's different than those sedimentary ones," she said.

Mrs. Weldon sat back in her chair, seeming to really look at Willie Mae for the first time. "It is. That's called igneous. It's created when molten rock, or magma, cools." She waved her hand toward a second box. "That type can go in there."

"Since there are three boxes, there must be three kinds of rocks," Willie Mae said. "What's the third called?"

"Metamorphic." Mrs. Weldon patted the dark stone with the white swirls in it in front of her. " 'Metamorphosis' means 'change.' These are rocks that are changed by the earth's pressure or heat."

Willie Mae reached for a rock that looked like a slice of the creek bank, all different shades of mud layered together. "Is this metamorphic?" she asked. She tried to imagine where you might find such a rock. Where Mrs. Weldon had found all of these rocks. It must have taken her a long time to gather up such a collection.

"What do you think?" Mrs. Weldon replied sharply.

Willie Mae's answer was to place it in the third box. Soon, she had a rhythm going, hefting rocks, looking them over carefully, and deciding which box to place them in. It was like the game she used to play with Mary Rose and Ma's button box, sorting the buttons by size or color or shape. Mrs. Weldon twitched like the cat that didn't catch the mouse when Willie Mae got them all sorted to a T.

"That's the last one." Willie Mae dropped the final knobby rock into the "sedimentary" box.

"Bring me that box there." Mrs. Weldon snapped her fingers impatiently.

Willie Mae took the box she'd indicated from the shelf. "Oh!" she said, startled.

"What is it?" Mrs. Weldon asked. "Spider?"

"No. No." Willie Mae held the box to her chest, all the while looking into the darkest eyes she'd ever seen. They belonged to a good-sized doll, likely hinged at the hips from the way she was sitting on the shelf.

Even though the doll had been partially hidden behind the box, Willie Mae was hard-pressed to figure how she had so far missed something this spectacular.

The doll looked like a princess, in a bright silk gown the color of wild persimmons, sprayed with blue flowers. Her long dark hair was sleek and smooth where Willie Mae's was wavy. Her lips were painted red, like those magazine ladies. Two hands like calla lilies rested in graceful crescents at her sides. Everything about her was exotic and fine. Willie Mae had never been one for dollies, but this one seemed to speak to her with those mysterious dark eyes. Willie Mae longed to brush the silk gown, run her fingers along the ribs of the faded paper parasol.

✳

Finally, the child has seen me. She's a scruffy-looking one. Thin, too. She holds her own with the old lady, doesn't back down. I have enjoyed listening to her read, but on the underside of her voice I hear the longing to tell her own stories. There's something else I hear, something troubling. It puts me in mind of peony blossoms, how they fade quickly when cut for the vase. Or the ragged edges of Master Tatsuhiko's words when he spoke of his little daughter.

I wish Brigitte were here. She would help me understand this puzzle.

✳

That face held Willie Mae's gaze. The parted lips made it look as if the doll was on the verge of saying something. And not just any something, like "How do you do?" or "Fine weather we're having." This doll, Willie Mae knew, would have stories to tell—of her faraway land and the people who lived there. Stories that would put Willie Mae's scribblings to shame.

Willie Mae glanced over at the old lady, whose head drooped toward her chest. Thinking her asleep emboldened Willie Mae to reach out and stroke the doll's shiny hair.

How foolish she is to compare my stories with hers. The wren and the nightingale sound nothing alike, but think how dull the world would be without the songs of both birds. Perhaps it is because she is a child that she does not comprehend this.

＊

"That's real hair, you know."

Willie Mae dropped her hand to her side. "I didn't mean no harm."

Mrs. Weldon pushed herself up out of her lady's chair and hobbled close enough that Willie Mae could smell her lily of the valley toilet water. "Real hair."

The apple-core face wrinkled into a frown. Mrs. Weldon tottered even closer and smoothed an imaginary wrinkle from the doll's dress. "Nonsense, at my age, buying a doll." She plucked a lacy handkerchief from her dress's sleeve and poked at her nose. "I went to that auction for a megalodon tooth. Fine specimen. Museum quality." She finished with her nose and tucked the handkerchief back into her sleeve. "Lord knows what came over me, but when they put this doll up on the block, she practically told me to bid. I swan. Something in those eyes of hers spoke to me." Her own eyes were drawn to the doll's then, just as Willie Mae's had been. Then she shook herself, as if surprised at what she'd said. "Of course, I know a doll couldn't tell me to do anything. It's not possible." She grabbed Willie Mae's arm and held on like a bulldog. "You won't prattle about this to my daughter?"

Willie Mae drew a cross over her heart. "I promise." The pressure on her arm lessened. "Those eyes pulled me right in, too. As if she was trying to tell me something." Willie Mae laughed. "Though, if she could talk, don't you think her stories would be something to hear? She could tell us how folks in Japan do things, what they like to eat and such."

Mrs. Weldon appraised the girl. So, she had an imagination, a desire to learn. She recalled another child like that, from long ago.

"You wear an old lady out with such ideas. You want me to have a stroke?" Mrs. Weldon took an exaggerated breath. "Help me back to my chair."

Willie Mae offered her arm and assisted Mrs. Weldon across the room. Once she was seated, Mrs. Weldon snapped her fingers for Willie Mae to pour her a glass of water, which she did.

Seated and refreshed, Mrs. Weldon resumed the story about the auction, ending with "So in addition to a bit of a dinosaur, I came home with a bit of the Orient. But"— she set her water glass down with a clink—"I don't feel I did too badly in the bargain."

She was quiet for so long, Willie Mae thought she'd nodded off to sleep again. Then Mrs. Weldon snapped, "She's got a name, you know. Miss Kanagawa."

"Miss Ka-na-ga-wa." Willie Mae tried it out. "That's a tongue tangler, for certain."

Mrs. Weldon laughed, right out loud. It was a sharp sound, like rocks clacking against one another when Cut Shin Creek was on the rise. "It surely is. A tongue tangler." She settled herself. "And a mind tangler, too. Heaven knows why I brought her home. But I find there's a reason for most happenings, even those that seem positively mysterious. What do you think?" She lifted the lid of the cut-glass candy dish next to her chair and selected a chocolate.

Willie Mae pondered a moment. "Preacher says Pap was taken to spare him further suffering here on earth. But Ma said what about *our* suffering, without a pap?" The sweet smell of chocolate distracted her from the conversation. She swallowed back the saliva in her mouth. "I admire Preacher, yes I do, but Ma seems to have a point."

Mrs. Weldon popped the chocolate into her mouth and chewed prodigiously. Willie Mae's jaws moved in time. The cut-glass lid clinked open again. Willie Mae fancied nibbling off one corner of such a candy. She imagined sweet chocolate warming her mouth. Another nibble and she would taste coconut. She was sure of that.

Mrs. Weldon ate another chocolate. All in one big bite. "I see your point. Your ma's point, that is." With her little finger, she rearranged something in her back teeth and smacked. "Well taken. Well taken." She swallowed, sniffed, then waved her hand. "Do you want to wear an old lady out? Leave me be, won't you?"

Willie Mae stumbled through a curtsy to Mrs. Weldon and stole a last look at Miss Kanagawa.

117

Tell your own stories.

✳

Willie Mae waved at the air by the side of her head. A mosquito or gnat must've gotten inside—what else could be teasing at her ear? That buzzing sounded almost like real words. But Mrs. Weldon's eyes were already shuttered up for her afternoon nap. Willie Mae's mind must be playing tricks on her.

She suddenly had the urge to get upstairs to her room and write something. Maybe even a poem about being able to munch on chocolates whenever you pleased. Of course, if Willie Mae had such a cut-glass dish full of sweets, she'd share.

This was only woolgathering, nothing more. There would be no sweets in the tote at the end of her month. Her hard-earned dollars would go toward a ham, some coffee, and soup beans. If there was something to jingle left over, it would go toward a packet of sugar for Ma's coffee. There was no room for such nonsense as store-bought chocolates in her future.

> *Dear Theo,*
>   *Mrs. Trent gave me a stamp so I could write you. Everyone here treats me real fine, even Mrs. Weldon, in her own way. She reminds me of that old hound of Pap's. Remember Copper? How he'd growl*

at us kids even when we were bringing him his
supper? He never did more than growl, but growl he
must. That's kind of like Mrs. Weldon. I imagine I'd
be a bit porcupiney myself, were I confined to my
bedroom after having traveled the world around.

Her room is such a glorious hodgepodge of
wonders, it would take weeks to study it all. That's
why I didn't even lay eyes on the Japanese doll until
today. She is something, Theo, dressed so fine and
with a face that makes her look most real. I swear
that some midnight she might up and speak, like the
animals did in that story you used to tell me. She has
inspired me to write a poem. If I get it into fair
enough shape, I will copy it out in my best hand and
send it to you.

Your loving sister,
Willie Mae

As she lay in bed that night, Willie Mae fought a puzzling achiness in her head and chest. She did miss Ma and Marvel and even baby Franklin, but this was something different. More in her body than in her heart. She tossed and turned, trying to find some ease. Comfort came finally when she imagined a tiny hand, soft and white as a lily, stroking her cheek until the stars, and then sleep, took over the night.

Miz Junkins stopped by the next morning. "I can't stay; I've got a long route today. But I wanted to see how things were going."

"We are getting along real good," Willie Mae said. "And I'm reading her *Tom Sawyer*!"

Miz Junkins exchanged a glance with Olive, who was standing behind Willie Mae in the doorway.

"You'd never believe it, Sarah." Olive wiped her hands on a dish towel. "This girl's like tonic for that old—I mean, for Mrs. Weldon."

They chatted a few more minutes and then Miz Junkins went on her way.

"You scarcely touched your biscuits," said Olive, frowning over Willie Mae's breakfast plate.

"I'll save them for dinner." Willie Mae didn't have much appetite. Maybe she was just that eager to run up to Mrs. Weldon's room. The old lady's tongue was as sharp as Ma's sewing shears, but her stories! She had lived. She had traveled. Willie Mae would have borne heaps of words sharp as needles in order to listen to Mrs. Weldon's yarns. She'd ridden a camel in Egypt and hunted pheasants with a duke in Austria.

"After my husband passed, I made up my mind not to let one moment go by without living life to the fullest," she'd told Willie Mae. The day she described her trip to Peru, Willie Mae had a headache herself thinking about fighting for a good breath in those high, high mountains with their thin, thin air.

Miz Junkins stopped by for a real visit one afternoon during Willie Mae's third week. "You feeling all right?" she asked. "You look a little peaked."

Willie Mae shook off the question. "I dreamt last night about pyramids. Did you know Mrs. Weldon's been to Egypt? And Spain? And that she dug for fossils in Peru?"

Miz Junkins poured a cup of tea from the pot Olive had prepared. "I had heard some such." She added a teaspoon of sugar and took a sip, satisfied now that a bit of pink had sprung into Willie Mae's cheeks. "How'd *Tom Sawyer* make out?"

"Oh, it was the best book I ever read!" Willie Mae dunked an icebox cookie into her own teacup. "That is, until we started reading about Huck Finn." She bit off the soggy sliver of cookie and swallowed. It scraped the entire way down her gizzard. Must've taken too big a bite. She swallowed again. "Miz Weldon has more books in that room of hers than a hound dog's got fleas."

Miz Junkins laughed. "Well, our library could surely use some of those fleas."

Willie Mae didn't hold Miz Junkins to fault for her comment. She'd learned from Olive that the liveliest topic in town was what would happen with all of Mrs. Weldon's impressive possessions after she passed.

The gossip held that Mrs. Weldon planned to leave her collections—including her books—to the Natural History Museum, in Lexington. What was left of her husband's money would be divided between her daughter and the Daughters of the American Revolution.

Willie Mae didn't like to think about such, even though she knew everyone died sometime. Still, she did lie awake a night or two wondering about Miss Kanagawa.

The fossils and shells and the like at the Natural History Museum would hardly be suitable company for her. Miss Kanagawa would prefer to be with people, plain and simple. Why, any doll would. Willie Mae could tell by the way those dark eyes seemed to warm up, like embers after you blew on them, when she went to Mrs. Weldon's room. Willie Mae took another sip of tea to soothe her throat. Where the doll would land after Mrs. Weldon was gone was something she'd never heard speculation about. She dunked her cookie again, determining to say her prayers this very night that it would be a long, long time until the doctor came up to the great door of this house, black bag in hand.

It wasn't that the Good Lord didn't heed Willie Mae's prayers in general. It was this latest one He paid no nevermind to. That very night, the doctor pounded at the great front door. The house lights were all aglow as he stamped his feet on the Aubusson rug in the front hall. "Take me to the patient," he said.

Though Olive answered his knock, it was Mrs. Trent who showed him up the stairs. He started right, toward Mrs. Weldon's room, but Mrs. Trent stopped him. "That way," she said, pointing to the stairs Olive was now climbing.

Mrs. Weldon opened her bedroom door, peering out. "I told you she'd bring the plague into this house. I told you she'd be trouble." She leaned hard against her walking stick.

"I sincerely doubt it's the plague," Dr. Pemberton said

evenly, easing his ample body around the bend in the landing. "The influenza's more like it. Going round up in the hills. Most likely that's what's ailing her."

"It's a plague all the same."

"Mrs. Weldon, why don't you let me see to the little one and we'll go from there?" Dr. Pemberton climbed the stairs and firmly shut the door between him and the old lady below. "Well, hello there, Willie Mae. How are you?"

He received no answer from the bed. Crossing the room in a manner completely unexpected for a man of his girth, he was at her side in an instant, one hand on her forehead, one on her wrist for her pulse. He took notice of Olive, in the corner, wringing a tea towel in her hands.

"This is no time for faint hearts," he told her, proceeding to rattle off a list of instructions for the pale patient's care. At the conclusion of his commands, he paused, brushing back the small girl's unruly hair from her face. "These holler children don't have much in reserve. But we will do our best."

Olive flew into action to carry out the doctor's orders. For the next few days, the household moved through its normal course, but always there was one ear cocked toward the tiny upstairs room.

"Why is my luncheon late again?" complained Mrs. Weldon on Tuesday.

"It has been ages since I've heard *Huck Finn*," she grumbled on Friday.

"All this fuss over a small girl," she clucked the Tuesday next. "What about me? I'm feeling quite faint."

"Have an egg," said Mrs. Trent, carrying in a breakfast tray. "It will bolster you up." She set the tray on the small table in her mother's room but didn't stay to crack or peel the egg on it. "Oh, I think I hear her coughing." She grabbed a pitcher of ice water and flew to the stairs.

"Well, I never." Mrs. Weldon pushed the soft-boiled egg aside and ate three pieces of toast with butter and apricot jam. It was a breakfast that would probably send her into diabetic shock. Severe diabetic shock.

But she was still on her feet at noon. "Where's my meal?" She rang for Olive.

"In a moment, ma'am." Olive flew past her, up the stairs to the room of that girl, bearing a tray with bouillon and sugar toast.

"I am on my last legs!" Mrs. Weldon called after her. But there was no answer. "I suppose I must starve in my own home." She pressed her right hand to her left breast. "Or die alone. All alone." Feeling abandoned and forlorn, she moved around her room, touching this object and that, taking complete inventory.

Her hand came to rest on a small speckled stone on the windowsill. She recalled the morning that Willie Mae had named the Egg Stone and held it to her ear. "Yep," she'd said. "I can hear some kind of rock baby in there, pecking its way out." She'd laughed at her silliness. Thinking of that laughter brought a sad smile to Mrs. Weldon's own lips. Even in the dreary days of December, her room had felt full of light and springtime. Ever since that girl had arrived.

She paused in front of Miss Kanagawa.

"Well, I suppose if you could speak, you'd be in a dither about her, like the rest of this household. Everything topsy-turvy." She fussed with the knot in the doll's obi. "In my day, children weren't allowed to cause a fuss. Such demands for attention would be met with the business end of a switch."

At that moment, she looked at the doll. Really looked at her, as she had the day of the auction.

❇

This old woman needs my help or her heart will shrivel up completely like a dried plum. My sway over adults is limited, though she heard me when I encouraged her to bid at the auction. Something in those cautious eyes told me she was the one I should go with.

Thank goodness she heard me then. But will she hear me now?

She was a child once, herself, was she not? Perhaps I need remind her of that child.

I sense a sickroom in her own past. And something else. Plums? No. Not plums. Another fruit.

❇

Into Mrs. Weldon's room from somewhere wafted the summertime fragrance of apricots. Not just any apricots, but the Moorparks that her mother had lovingly tended. She remembered being about the same age as that holler girl, carrying a brown transferware bowl full of them up to her mother's sickroom when her father stopped her with news that sent the bowl shattering to the floor.

After her mother's death, she followed her father's lead and turned inward, determined to be sufficient unto herself. That attitude had stood her in good stead throughout her life. Until recently.

It seemed everyone thought her selfish, including her own daughter. She'd learned too late that friends needed cultivating, too, like her beloved mother's apricot trees. Solitary in her room, she'd had nothing to do but take inventory of her increasing aches and pains, wondering if the next inhale would be her last. Of course, there hadn't been much time for such since Willie Mae had come to stay.

She caught her breath after this particular thought. She found she couldn't remember the last time she'd had a headache or a neck ache or any sort of ache. For years, she'd felt like a neglected pocket watch tossed in a drawer. Since Willie Mae's arrival, she'd felt properly wound up, in tune and ready to tick.

All because of an urchin from the holler. She glanced at the doll. "Her name's Willie Mae," she said. "I didn't care for it at first, but it suits her. Sharp little thing, too. And not a bad reader. Reads almost as eloquently as I do." She tapped her cheek with her forefinger. *That* was the ticket. Nothing like a read-aloud to send the punies flying. She herself knew that firsthand. Mrs. Weldon searched for the copy of *Huckleberry Finn*. Then she recalled she'd let the girl—let Willie Mae—take it to her room.

"Never let it be said that Ernestine Weldon does not have a Christian bone in her body," she declared. She would visit the child. Comfort her. Bring her succor.

Mrs. Weldon refreshed herself—washing face, combing hair, reanointing with her favorite toilet water—then prepared to venture out of her own room and up to the child's. It was the farthest she'd been in . . . Well, she couldn't remember in how long. But surely a woman who had ascended Machu Picchu in her youth could climb a set of stairs in her own home.

She grabbed her walking stick and started for the door.

Something pulled her back. One took something to the ill, did one not? It was out of season for apricots, certainly. What could she take?

She glanced around her room, ajumble with the detritus of her unconventional life, looking for an appropriate sickroom gift. Her eyes landed on just the thing. She galumphed across the floor, gathered up the target of her gaze, and started for the stairs. It felt as if she were back on Machu Picchu, earning each step, her lungs struggling for each sip of oxygen. But after a small eternity, she was at the landing, thumping her way up the stairs.

"Mrs. Weldon!" Olive scurried to meet her at the door. "What? How?" She gathered her apron and her thoughts about her. "It's not wise for you to come in."

"Pish posh." Mrs. Weldon tapped her stick on the floor by Olive's feet, scaring the woman out of her way. "She's only a child."

"A very ill child, and you are—" Olive stopped in midsentence.

"A very old lady." Mrs. Weldon progressed into the room. "What of it?" She shifted the object she toted to her other arm. "Move aside." She clumped toward the bed.

"Willie Mae, we are behind in *Huckleberry Finn*." She peered at the pale face, paler than the pillowcase on which it lay. "At this rate we shall not finish before your time is up." Her hand flew to her cheek. "I mean, before it is time for you to return home."

"Mrs. Weldon—" Olive stepped forward as if to pull the older lady out of the room.

The girl stirred. Coughed. Coughed again. "I'm sorry, ma'am," Willie Mae offered in a voice as wispy as an angel's robe. "I aim to be up soon." As if to prove the point, she struggled to sit up under the coverlet.

"Stay down!" Mrs. Weldon commanded her. "It's no sense you reading to me now, anyway. Your voice would sound like a cat scratching on a mirror. I will read, if you tell me where you've placed the book. Oh"—with weary arms, she held out the object she'd been carrying—"and I need you to do something for me. I need you to watch over Miss Kanagawa while I, while I . . ." She glanced at Olive. "While I go to Lexington for an important appointment. There's no one else I trust." She stepped so close to the bed that she could smell the mustard poultice Olive had recently applied. "May I have your word

128

you'll keep her safe?" She placed the doll in the bed next to Willie Mae, whose tears dried the moment she gazed feverishly into its eyes.

Mrs. Weldon turned to Olive. "Where is the doctor?" she hissed. "This child needs care!"

"He's stopping back this evening," Olive said. She moved to the bed, smoothing the coverlet, smoothing the child's hair.

Mrs. Weldon fluffed herself up like a broody hen. "I should think so." She reached her hand out, too, as if to touch Willie Mae's hair.

"I'll stay with her, Mrs. Weldon," said Olive. "You best go back to your room."

Mrs. Weldon tapped her cane on the floor. "And you'd best mind your own business." She scanned the room. "Ah, there's *Huck Finn,* over there." She moved toward the bureau and snatched the book from its resting place on top. She spied a rocking chair in the corner and hobbled toward it.

Settling into the chair, Mrs. Weldon opened the book up smartly.

A slip of paper fell into her lap. "I could do with a glass of water, Olive. With a thin slice of lemon," she added, picking up the paper.

Olive sighed loudly, nodded, and slipped out of the room.

Mrs. Weldon glanced at the page in her hands. It was rough and coarse, with many erasures and written in a child's round hand. The sheet was filled with poems—about giant seashells and river rafts and sorting stones. The very last poem was entitled "A Quiet Friend, by Willie Mae Marcum." Mrs. Weldon glanced over at the girl, now sound asleep with her thin arms wrapped tight around the very subject of the poem. Softly, she read the last stanza aloud:

> She hasn't told me with her words,
> That doll with hands as graceful as birds,
> But I know by looking into her eyes so dark
> That she counts me friend within her heart.

Mrs. Weldon read all of the poems, and found her eyes misty at their sweetness. There was even one about *her*, comparing their daily visits to pulling treasures out of a Christmas stocking. Mrs. Weldon was not a frivolous woman, but she would have been willing to bet that no one—except perhaps her beloved Arthur—would look at time spent with her in such a way. She pushed herself out of the rocker and limped over to the child's bed. Should her forehead be so hot? Her cheeks so pale? She was going to give Dr. Pemberton a piece of her mind when he arrived.

As she watched the girl, an image of her young self came to mind, and a humiliating memory of her father finding some of the poems she'd written after Mother's death and reading them aloud over supper one night. She sensed that Willie Mae wasn't ready to share these with the world yet, either, so she refolded the paper and tucked it under Miss Kanagawa's obi as the doll lay in the sleeping girl's arms. The poems would be safe until Willie Mae was up and around again. Mrs. Weldon made her way back to the rocker, determining that after *Huck Finn*, they should read poetry. She had that lovely collection of Wordsworth, for starters, and then they could move on. Perhaps to Dickinson or maybe even that Yankee, Robert Frost.

When Olive returned with Mrs. Weldon's glass of water, the old lady didn't pay her any mind. She kept reading out loud from that *Huck Finn* book. She read all night, even after Dr. Pemberton came. She read and read and read, from one day to the next, until that little girl slipped out of the suffering of this world and flew on angel's wings to meet her Pap and Mary Rose.

Though she could never see the reason in it and it exasperated her no end, Mrs. Weldon lived for five years more, during which time she arranged for a monthly check to be delivered to Willie Mae's family—something not even the nosiest of the town's busybodies ever discovered.

After Mrs. Weldon died, Sarah Junkins nearly fell off her horse when Mrs. Trent flagged her down and told her she'd been left the Weldon book collection along with strict orders to open a free lending library. And the mayor got a nice check to build said library. That was surprise enough, but the whole town was knocked for a loop when it was revealed that Mrs. Weldon had not, after all, left any money to the Daughters of the American Revolution, but instead had bequeathed a tidy sum to her daughter, and to a family she'd never met, way down Cut Shin Creek.

✳

MISS KANAGAWA

After the little girl died, I tried my best to comfort the old woman. On good days, I was able to untangle some pleasant memories from her sad thoughts and pull them to the surface. Then she would speak to me. "Remember when Willie Mae made that joke about the Egg Rock?" she might say. Or, "I knew that girl was something special the first day she read to me from *Tom Sawyer*." Or, "Didn't Willie Mae's smile light up this sorry old room like fireworks on the Fourth of July?" For a few fleeting moments, she was lifted by such remembrances. But nothing could truly bend her grief; it was rigid as a *yari*, a spear.

Most times the old woman sent everyone away. She would rock sorrowfully in her chair, a copy of *Huckleberry Finn* in her lap, saying nothing. It was impossible for me to connect with her. There on the shelf, I was left to my own thoughts.

I came to understand that those unfamiliar twinges inside me when I met Bunny and Lois were part of the awakening process. Those little discomforts were signs that the tight bud of my heart had begun its slow unfurling into full bloom. But I do not understand why Master Tatsuhiko wished this awakening for me. I do not know why any doll would want it, not when it means being opened to the pain of loss.

And yet, that pain is softened somewhat when I recall that my presence dried many of Willie Mae's tears. I think I now understand Master Tatsuhiko's words about good and bad being entwined in one rope.

Though I wish I did not.

＊

Lucy Turner

Lucy balanced the tablet on her bent knees, writing furiously to block out the hum of grown-up voices downstairs. It had been only a week, but Mama's scent was disappearing from Aunt Miriam's house. The best place to smell Mama anymore was here, in the bedroom closet. The closet was a good place for other reasons, too. When Lucy was inside it, she could block out the face Pop was wearing these days, all ragged and gray like a worn-out sock. She could block out all the people downstairs, in the kitchen, dressed in somber suits and somber dresses. She could even block out Aunt Miriam, wearing a flowered apron as she served sandwiches and coffee.

In the closet, no one bothered Lucy with words that

didn't make any sense, like "She's gone to a better place" or "At least she's not suffering anymore."

In the closet, she could let out the tears that came every time she thought about Mama going to the hospital, and not coming back. She scribbled furiously.

Dear Mrs. Roosevelt,

    Even though I haven't gotten an answer to my last letter, I wanted to write and let you know about Mama. It hurts to breathe sometimes when I think of this world without her. I had hoped to get a new dress for the funeral. But we made do. Gloria Jean's big sister had outgrown her Easter dress and it fit me pretty good after Aunt Miriam shortened it and tied the bow in back extra tight.

    Pop says you are too busy to answer all the letters you get, but in case you have time to answer mine, I wanted to let you know that we are leaving Goodwell soon. We are headed for Californ-i-a, where Pop is sure to get work. I will write again to let you know our address.

Your friend,
Lucy Turner

She put her pencil and tablet down, wiggling deeper into the closet, the hem of Mama's waltzing dress brushing the top of her head. Lucy could almost imagine it was a dancing night, a Friday night, again and Mama was calling to her, "Lucy, come tie the bow on the back of this dress. You're the only one who can get it just so."

"Midget?"

Lucy raised her head at Pop's voice, saw that he held out a plate. "It's red velvet cake. Your favorite."

She ducked her head again, rubbing tears against her scratchy stockings so he wouldn't see. The last cake Mama had baked was a red velvet cake for Lucy's ninth birthday last month. "I'm not hungry."

Pop eased to the floor, just outside the door frame. She heard the clink of china against the linoleum. "Me either."

When she turned her head to peek at him, he patted the floor by his leg. She hesitated, then scooted out from the closet and under his arm. Pop rested his chin on her head. Lucy breathed in his smell of tobacco and coffee and St. John's Bay Rum aftershave.

"The preacher did a real fine job today, didn't he?"

Lucy nodded in agreement.

"Real fine," Pop repeated. Lucy could feel his heart beating hard in his chest. "Your mama would've loved the singing, too." His voice cinched up and he didn't speak for a while. Lucy didn't mind; it was a comfort to sit with him without having to say anything. Mama had been the talker in their family, anyway. She would chatter like a kingbird trying to scare folks away from its nest. But it was lively chatter, happy chatter. Any story Mama told was bright and cheery, like the first jonquils in spring. Thinking about her made Lucy's throat clamp tight and her eyes all leaky.

"I got something important to talk to you about." Pop's chin bobbed up and down on her head as he spoke.

She snuggled closer.

He cleared his throat. "Aunt Miriam—" he started. Then he scratched his neck. "A girl needs a woman around. And Aunt Miriam could sure keep you comfortable. Better than sleeping in our old jalopy on the road."

Lucy pushed herself away so she could look her father in the face. "No. No. I'm going with you." That was the one thing she'd held on to through Mama's long sickness, through losing the farm, through having to move to Aunt Miriam's, with her unhappy ways and constant reminders that they were living off her charity. California meant a home of their own again. She wasn't going to lose that chance. "No sir, no way. I'm not staying."

Pop patted his pocket for his pipe and tobacco. But he left them there. Aunt Miriam threw conniptions about his smoking in the house. "There's liable to be tough times. Empty bellies."

"Times won't be so tough if we're together. Besides, you said a man couldn't go hungry in California. Beans and pears and tomatoes and potatoes. It's a regular Garden of Eden, you said." Back on their farm, ankle deep in dust, Pop had sat at the kitchen table, night after night, reading aloud to her and to Mama from handbills printed by the growers in California. The flyers said things like "300 workers needed for peaches. Plenty of work. Start Right Away." After the last cow died, they'd made plans to head west right then and there. As soon as Mama felt better.

But she didn't get better.

138

"I know I said that, but—" Pop took off his glasses and rubbed his eyes. He pushed his specs back up on his nose. "You'd have to leave Gloria Jean."

Lucy couldn't remember a day when Gloria Jean hadn't been in her life. But if she had to choose between Pop and Gloria Jean . . . "Well, we can write. And maybe her family will come west, too. She said her daddy's talking about it."

Pop let out a breath, long and slow. "I never could win an argument with either of my girls." He hugged Lucy. "Okay, partner. I'll tell Aunt Miriam." He stood up, brushed off his trousers, and headed downstairs.

Lucy reached for the plate Pop had brought her and ate up the slice of cake, every last crumb.

Pop did odd jobs—mostly for Aunt Miriam, who was practically the only person in Goodwell who hadn't gone bust—for a month or so to earn the money to fix up their Model A for the trip. Lucy and he spent hours poring over maps of Route 66, the "Mother Road," which would take them to California. "Wouldn't it be something to see the ocean?" Lucy asked. She dreamed of scuffing her bare feet on wet sand, chasing after waves, filling her pockets with shells.

"Don't think we'll make it that far west," said Pop. He had it all planned out—they'd cut down through Texas and pick cotton around about Amarillo. "That should fit us up to get to someplace in Arizona for the lettuce and carrots. I might could earn some real money that would carry us through to California."

"I'm a good picker," Lucy said. She pumped her right arm to show her muscles. She'd helped in the fields at the farm since she could walk.

"You are, at that," Pop agreed. He lit his pipe and moved out to Aunt Miriam's front porch to smoke. She had fussed at him something awful after that cinder from his pipe had burned a hole in her settee.

"Can I go see Gloria Jean?" Lucy followed him out, holding the map. "And show her where we're going?"

Pop nodded.

That was the best thing about having moved off the farm and into town to live with Aunt Miriam. Gloria Jean was now only two streets away. Lucy was a fast runner and was knocking at Gloria Jean's front door in no time. The two girls plopped on the parlor floor, studying the map.

"It looks like a long ways," Gloria Jean said in a small voice. "Farther than I thought."

"That's why you have to talk your daddy into coming, too." Lucy traced her finger along Route 66. For her, it wasn't so much a road as a magic carpet that would carry them far away from dust and despair to a place where it was warm and sunny and she'd eat oranges until the juice ran down her legs and filled her shoes. Because she *would* have shoes in California. Everybody did.

"Where should we live when we get to California? Bakersfield? Wasco? Lamont?" Lucy's pointer finger jumped around on the map.

"'Lamont' has a nice friendly sound," Gloria Jean said, twisting her pigtail around her finger.

Lucy nodded in agreement. "It does, doesn't it?" She drew an imaginary circle around the town of Lamont. "That's it, then. Lamont. We'll get there first and check it out so that when you come, we can show you all around."

Gloria Jean was as still as the air before a storm. Then she rolled off her stomach and onto her back. "It's a nice dream, Lucy. I sure hope it comes true." Her words wobbled a bit, as if they were having to work their way around some tears.

"It's got to, Gloria Jean. It's just got to." Lucy rolled onto her back, too, tapping her left foot against Gloria Jean's right. Then she sat straight up. "Let's make a pact. A friendship pact."

Gloria Jean wiped her eyes, then nodded. "Okay. But what shall it be?"

Lucy bit her lip, thinking. "I've got it." She began to untie the ribbon from her pigtail and motioned for Gloria Jean to do the same. "I'll always wear one of your ribbons and you always wear one of mine. That way, every morning, no matter how far apart we are, we'll think of each other."

They made the switch, then stood in front of the mirror, studying two sets of pigtails, each set with one green ribbon and one blue.

"We'll be friends forever," said Gloria Jean, touching the new ribbon in her hair.

"This old world isn't big enough to keep us two friends

apart." Lucy tilted her head so it touched the side of Gloria Jean's. "Sister Gloria Jean, can I get an amen to that?"

Gloria Jean sniffled and laughed at the same time. "Amen, Sister Lucy. Amen."

❋

There came a time when the old woman's room was quiet, empty. I was bundled up into my trunk, along with my belongings. And there I slept until yesterday, when I was brought into the light again. Before I knew Willie Mae, it would have been mortifying to hear the list of my shortcomings as I was lifted from my trunk: "Look how worn this kimono is" and "Can we get that mark off her obi?" and "I don't know if we can fix that dirty spot on her cheek."

Now I wear such scars with pride.

❋

With Pop already behind the wheel and raring to go, Lucy jumped out of the car. "I forgot something!" She ran back inside Aunt Miriam's house for her tablet and pencil. How would she have kept up with her letter writing if they'd been left behind? She grabbed them and hurried back to the car.

"You finally ready?" Pop asked her, double-clutching, and easing the gear stick into first.

Lucy hugged her tablet to her chest. She kept her eyes focused straight ahead and didn't let them veer anywhere near the direction of Gloria Jean's house. "Yes. I'm ready."

Pop pushed old Betsy's horn. *AAOOOGAH!*

AAOOOGAH! "And they're off," he said, mimicking the horse race announcer he sometimes listened to on the radio.

"And *we're* off," Lucy corrected.

Pop answered her by launching into a rousing rendition of "California, Here I Come": "That's why I can hardly wait, Open up that Golden Gate, California, here I come!"

After they'd sung the song through three times, Lucy scrunched around in her seat and peeked over the boxes and bedding in the back to try to catch a glimpse of Goodwell out the rear window. She couldn't see anything. Anything at all. It was almost as if Goodwell were only a place in her imagination. That it never existed, that wonderful place she was born, grew up in. The place she'd always be from.

Mixed-up feelings bounced around in her belly as the car bounced over the rough road. She'd wanted to move west, especially after Mama passed. It was their chance for a real home again, not living with relatives. Even if they had to live in a town, not on a farm, she thought it might help her and Pop to heal over their big sore. Not that they'd ever get over losing Mama. That was impossible. But Lucy'd got it in her head that California would soothe their hearts a bit. Now, driving away, all she could think about was Mama's little grave, lonesome back there in the Goodwell Pioneer Cemetery, with only a cross made from the staves of an old feed bucket to mark it. Pop had told Reverend Parker that as soon as he got the money together, he'd send it along for a proper stone. She and Pop had already picked out what it would say: *Lila Lucille Turner, A True Prairie Flower, May 10, 1907–August 5, 1939.*

Lucy said the words aloud: "A true prairie flower."

"What's that?" Pop asked. It was hard to carry on a conversation, as the Model A had developed a cranky cough that Pop couldn't fix.

Lucy shook her head. "Nothing," she said, louder. She didn't figure Pop needed a reminder of Mama now, the very moment they were headed west.

Pop nodded, then took off his hat and tossed it in the back. They drove and drove and drove. Lucy fell asleep and woke up and fell asleep and woke up again as Pop eased old Betsy off onto the shoulder.

They ate the lunch Aunt Miriam had packed— hard-boiled eggs and biscuits and oatmeal cookies— washing it down with a thermos of sweet tea.

Pop wiped his mouth with the back of his hand. "I'm going to make this swallow last. It's going to be some time before we can spring for sugar in our tea."

Lucy sipped her tea from a dented tin cup. She would've preferred lemonade. Or sarsaparilla, which she'd had only once in her whole life. "How much longer till we cross the state line?" she asked.

"Now, if you're going to start that up, this trip will take an eternity." Pop unrolled his tobacco pouch and made himself a pipe. He puffed on it to get it going once it'd been lit, and then his face softened. "I expect it'll be close to suppertime."

Lucy nodded, then set about tidying up after their picnic while Pop finished his pipe. She visited the bushes on one side of the road, and Pop did the same on the other side. Then they were ready to start off again.

Settled back in the car and under way, she pulled out her tablet.

Pop glanced over at her. "You're not writing another letter to Mrs. Roosevelt, are you?"

Lucy grinned. "Gloria Jean," she said, hollering over the engine noise. It was tricky to write at first, but then she learned that if she just eased up all over her body and rode out the jounces and bounces like she was riding Pop's old horse, Ace, she could manage. She had just finished writing the words "Dear Gloria Jean" when a powerful jolt threw her clean off the seat onto the floor. "What was that?" She scrambled back up.

Pop fought to settle Betsy off to the side of the road. When she was stopped, he got out and took a look. "Tire," he said. He kicked at the flat. "Might as well get out and get yourself comfy while I patch it."

Lucy found a small clump of grass to sit on and picked up her tablet again.

Dear Gloria Jean,

We're already having our first adventure on the trip. After lunch, we got a flat tire. We thought we'd cross the state line around suppertime. I hope this won't put us too far behind.

Lucy chewed on the end of her pencil. There wasn't much else to tell Gloria Jean about the trip so far. It'd only been a few hours.

She watched Pop wrestle the tire off the rim and pull out the inner tube. "Hand me the patch kit, will you?" He leaned his cheek close to the tube, to feel where the air was escaping. "Grab the pump, too."

Lucy shifted a box of potatoes, a lard can filled with sugar-cured bacon, and the small pasteboard box with her clothes. "Here you go." She gave the supplies to her father, who pumped and pumped until he was satisfied. He pulled a tire gauge from his shirt pocket and checked the pressure. "I'd say we're ready to saddle up again." While he put the tire back on the rim, she put the tools away. It was well past suppertime when they rattled into Amarillo.

Near Amarillo, Texas
October 7, 1939

Dear Mrs. Roosevelt,

I bet you're surprised to hear from me again. We have been living in a tramp camp for the past few months, picking cotton for a farmer here in Amarillo. Sometimes I babysit for the farmer's wife. Yesterday she gave me five stamps as pay because she knows how much I like to write letters!

The tramp camp's not much but it's worked out fine. We can leave Betsy—that's what we call our Model A—put because it's only a mile or so to walk

*to the fields. Pop found some pasteboard and I found
some lard buckets and we've turned old Betsy into a
Ritz Hotel! It's like the forts Gloria Jean and I used to
build on the farm. When we had our farm.*

*I don't mean to keep bothering you with our
troubles, but it's time to be getting on our way and
we've had the bad luck of four flat tires. Pop's worried
that last patch won't hold us till we get to California,
so I was wondering if you could loan us $12.50 for a
new tire. We'll pay you back, I promise.*

*Your friend,
Lucy Turner*

Lucy checked with the farmer's wife, Mrs. Foley, one
last time before they left Amarillo. Mrs. Foley shook her
head. "Sorry, Lucy. There was no letter today." She jiggled baby Vernon on her hip. Vernon reached out his
hands to Lucy.

"Show your mama 'Pat-a-Cake,'" Lucy said, putting
her hands over Vernon's chubby ones. "Pat-a-cake, pat-
a-cake, baker's man. Bake me a cake as fast as you can.
Pat it and roll it"—here she turned his little hands in a
circle—"and mark it with a V, and throw it in the oven for
Vernon and me!"

Vernon laughed and held out his hands. "Agin," he
said.

Lucy cooperated.

"Hang on to him a minute, will you?" Mrs. Foley
handed over the baby and hurried off. Lucy and Vernon

got through "Pat-a-Cake" two more times before Mrs. Foley came back with a lumpy flour sack. "Here's you some sandwiches and raisins and an onion and some beans. That'll take the crinks out of an empty stomach when you're down the road a bit."

Lucy took a step back. "Oh, I better not. Pop don't take charity."

Mrs. Foley clicked her tongue. "'Tisn't charity. It's your pay! For all them times you helped me with the baby." She pushed the sack at Lucy, who hesitated only a moment longer.

"Thank you, Mrs. Foley." Lucy handed Vernon to his mother and then took the flour sack. "I'll miss you and Vernon."

"There'll always be a job for your daddy here. You, too." Mrs. Foley walked her to the door.

"Pop says old Betsy will only go one direction on the Mother Road and that's west." Lucy's stomach grumbled at the smell of the onion in the sack. There'd been no breakfast this morning or supper last night. They were saving every penny, every crust of bread, for the next leg of their trip. "But I could write you."

Mrs. Foley nodded. "You do that. Let me know how you make out in sunny California."

When she got to the end of the walk, Lucy turned to wave. But Mrs. Foley and Vernon had gone back inside the house. That was no nevermind. Easier to say good-bye that way. She tossed the sack over her shoulder and didn't mind one bit how it caused her neck to ache on the walk back to the camp. Because what was inside would help take away the ache in her belly. At least for a little while.

Lucy and Pop were in good spirits as they sailed through Tucumcari, New Mexico. "Too bad we can't stop and stay awhile," Lucy said. "That name sounds like a song." Pop agreed, making up a little ditty that he sang loudly off-key: "To live in Tucumcari, you must be very hairy." As they were passing through Winslow, Arizona, the patched tube gave clean out. Pop steered the car to a parking spot in front of a bakery and then sat there for the longest time, his hands gripping the steering wheel, his head bowed. The smell of cinnamon and sugar and yeast made Lucy woozy. She swallowed hard, pretending she was swallowing a bite of one of those sweet rolls in the bakery window. Finally Pop shoved the driver's-side door open and got out. "Come on. We gotta find an inner tube."

He stopped a man wearing a suit coat over his overalls and was pointed to the hardware store a few blocks away. The store carried the inner tube Pop needed. And they had something else.

"Puppies!" Lucy exclaimed as Pop took out his paper-thin billfold. She scooped one of the spotted powder puffs up in her arms. The pup wiggled to get at her face to give it a good washing. "Look!" She held the puppy out so Pop could see its tiny black nose and kind eyes.

"Don't even ask!" The sharpness in Pop's voice nearly made Lucy drop the puppy.

*

I sit on the shelf, watching the seamstress mend my kimono. It seems I am being prepared for something, but I do not know what that is.

There is a new feeling in my heart—how strange and yet how sweet to say that word. It is a bit like being nudged awake by the sun, before it has even risen. Or like hearing a gentle tune on the wind, when there is no *yokobue,* no flute, in sight.

Or like there is a string tied to my heart, as if it is a kite being tugged by a kite flier whose face I cannot see.

Yet.

*

Lucy set the fluffball back in the cardboard box with its sign, "Free to Good Homes." "I wasn't going to ask for a puppy," she said quietly. It was tough enough to feed themselves; she knew they couldn't take on a pet. But what was the harm in cuddling this dog? For a short moment, the puppy's meaty breath, wet tongue, and soft fur had taken her away from this place and their troubles. Holding him, she'd felt almost as good as she had back when Mama was alive, when they still had the farm.

She ducked her head and slipped out of the store, waiting on a splintery bench out front while Pop paid for the inner tube. She was sure when he came out, he'd tell her he was sorry for snapping at her. It wasn't like Pop, who never raised his voice at her, not even when she burned the first batch of hotcakes she tried to cook.

But when Pop came out, he brushed past her without a word. She couldn't move, she was that surprised.

About ten steps away he stopped and called over his shoulder. "You coming?"

Biting her bottom lip to stop it from trembling, she eased off the bench and followed him back to old Betsy.

Holbrook, Arizona
November 20, 1939

Dear Gloria Jean,

I traded my hairbrush for some stamps so I can write you. Pop says no more letters to Mrs. Roosevelt and I promised. At least for a while.

We are in Holbrook, Arizona. Pop's picking lettuce and I'm pulling carrots. I made thirty-five cents yesterday! I know you have started up to school again. That's one thing I miss. But soon enough we'll be to California and I'll get into school there. In the meantime, one of the ladies here used to be a schoolteacher and she has let me borrow her copy of Little Women. *I would like to be Jo because she's so bold, but I think I'm more like Beth, who's quiet. I think I have a little more backbone than she does, though. The other day, the field boss gave me a nickel instead of the quarter I'd earned and I spoke right up. He frowned but made it right.*

What does your pop say about coming west? I sure miss you! I wear your ribbon every single day.

Friends forever,
Lucy

Lucy thought it would be the best present ever to roll across the California state line on Christmas Eve. Out of Kingman, Arizona, Route 66 had changed its temperament. Most of the way, the Mother Road had been easygoing and easy to maneuver, if a bit bumpy and lumpy now and again. Past Kingman, she got a sharpness to her. She'd turned all unfriendly, as if to say, "You want California? It'll cost you." The road went up and up and up, with steep grades that set Betsy to chugging. And the curves were as tight as Aunt Miriam's pin curls—without a guardrail in sight.

They'd skittered and rumbled their way a good part of the morning, but when the road leveled out a bit, Pop set the hand brake. "You best walk, Lucy." He nodded toward the back. "Carry that wash bucket and maybe your clothes. Gotta lighten the load."

Lucy didn't move at first, thinking the old Pop had come back and was pulling her leg. But she saw the ring of white around his mouth and the same white in his knuckles as he grasped the steering wheel, so she hopped to. She pulled out her box of clothes, the washtub, the coffeepot, and the cast-iron skillet. As Pop eased away, she also snagged a bit of rope from the backseat. Old Betsy's gears groaned as she lurched upward.

"Meet you at the top!" Pop called. Betsy was like a high-strung colt, skittish to think of climbing that hill. If anyone could get her up and over, it'd be Pop.

Lucy stood there, trying not to feel all alone in the world as Pop and Betsy bumped out of sight. She looked at the pile of belongings next to her and wondered how in the world she was going to carry them. Best thing to do was toss everything in the tub and drag it along with the rope, hoping she didn't wear a hole in it. She was tying the rope to the handle of the washtub when she heard a car chug-chugging up behind her. She yanked on the rope to pull her load out of its way.

Next thing she knew, a string bean of a boy was next to her, struggling with his own mess of stuff, and calling, "See ya soon," toward the car. A woman's voice called out, "Watch your brother!" Lucy saw that with the string bean was another boy, maybe four years old.

"Walking to the top?" the string bean asked.

She rolled her eyes. "Nope. I'm planning to fly."

He laughed out loud, showing a mouthful of missing teeth. "That's a good'un." He pointed at himself with his thumb. "I'm Winston. And this here's Wilson."

Lucy softened. There wasn't any call to be so snooty. Besides, with these two scarecrows at least she wouldn't be alone on the climb up. "I'm Lucy."

"Wilson doesn't say much," Winston said. "You might say I'm the mouth of the family. But he's the brains, and I can see he's got a plan."

Lucy looked at Wilson, whose eyes were barely visible under a shock of hair in bad need of cutting. He didn't look much like a mastermind to her. Not with that thumb in his mouth. "What's the plan?"

Wilson removed his thumb and pointed at the washtub. Winston translated.

"We stuff everythin' in the tub and you take one handle and I take the other. That way, we divide the load and multiply the joy." Winston grinned. Lucy couldn't help but grin back.

"That's a great idea, Wilson," she said. The little boy popped his thumb back in his mouth as his big brother and Lucy loaded their respective belongings into the tub.

"Heave ho!" said Winston, and they hefted the tub off the ground. Winston reminded Lucy of Mama, chattering away about this thing and that. She learned that they'd lost their farm, like Pop and Lucy, but in Nebraska. They were headed to their uncle's place in Bakersfield. "You should come, too," Winston said. "He needs lots of help picking his grapes. He's got the biggest farm around."

"Really?" Lucy motioned to Winston to hold up so she could pull a burr from her foot.

"Course." He threw his shoulders back. "He's my uncle, ain't he?"

All that long uphill trudge, the only breeze came from Winston's flapping lips. But Lucy didn't mind. The talk took her mind off her hot, sore feet and the muscles in her shoulders that grumbled so about toting that washtub.

The whole walk, Wilson didn't say a word. He toddled along behind them, bending every now and again to pick up a stone or a feather or some other roadside treasure. He didn't even exclaim when he found a penny—head up!—in the dust. He tapped at Lucy until she turned and he unfolded his grubby fingers.

"Well, this is your lucky day," she told him.

The corners of his mouth worked into a smile around his thumb. He held the penny tight in his left hand. Lucy understood that: every pocket she owned was more hole than pocket. She imagined that was the case for Wilson, too.

It was an hour or more that they went along. When they crested the hill, they found their parents leaning on Betsy's hood, talking like old friends. Lucy and Winston dropped the washtub and joined the adults. After introductions around, Lucy got herself a swig of water from the canteen, then thought to offer Winston and Wilson a swallow.

"Thanks, but we got a canteen ourselves." Winston jerked his thumb toward the back of their truck.

"Best of luck to you," Pop was saying, sticking his hand out to shake with Winston's father.

"Same to you. Remember—it's the Hoffman place. In Bakersfield. I'm sure my brother would have work for you." Winston's father shook Pop's hand, then slapped his hand on Betsy's fender. "She looks like she'll get you wherever you want to go," he said.

"I sure hope so." Pop pulled open the driver's-side door.

Lucy ran around to the passenger's side. "Bye, Winston. Bye, Wilson!"

Wilson's thumb popped out of his mouth. "Bye, Lucy."

She smiled and leaned out the window, waving at her hiking partners until she couldn't see anything but clouds of dust behind them.

She settled into her seat. She knew from studying the

155

map they still had to cross 140 miles of desert, but that was their last test. The last barrier between them and a new life in California. "California, here I come," she started to sing, but one look from Pop and she quieted down.

"We're not there yet," he said.

Lucy scrunched down in her seat, wishing they were there, wishing her old Pop—the one who would've been singing right along with her—was there, too.

March 25, 1940
Merrill FSA Camp,
Klamath County, Oregon

Dear Mrs. Roosevelt,

It's me again. I'm sure you're surprised that I'm writing from Oregon, not California. Well, it didn't work out the way we planned. The first thing we saw when we got to Bakersfield was a big sign saying "Okies Go Home." There were other signs, too, like "If You're Looking for Work, Keep Going." Pop didn't believe them. At first. Pop's a hard worker— me too—but there were no jobs to be had. And especially not for folks from Oklahoma. We packed up our hopes and headed north for Delano. Nothing there, either. Pop traded our coffeepot and washtub for enough gas to get to Tulare, but it was the same story. A farmer let us have a couple of heads of old cabbage, so we ate cabbage soup for two weeks straight. My stomach sure hopes we don't ever have

to do that again. A nice preacher told us about the
Farm Security Administration Camp at Tulare, but
Pop said he'd had enough of the great state of
California. Then the preacher told us about another
FSA camp, in Oregon. Pop sold his wedding ring for
gas money.

After sleeping on the ground for months, it was
real nice to get to Oregon and sleep in a tent on a
raised wood platform. We don't have the dollar a
week for our rent, so Pop's working it off around the
camp. That's what lots of the folks do.

You might think I'm writing to ask for something
again, but this time I am not. I'm writing to thank
you and President Roosevelt for putting up these
camps for us Okies. See, most other folks think we're
trash. I won't even write down some of the names
I've been called. But now there's a shower so I can be
clean and there's breakfast for us children for a penny
a day. I've had breakfast three times in one week! I'll
be so fat soon, I won't fit in my overalls.

> *Your friend,*
> *Lucy Turner*

After sleeping out in the open, on the side of the road, for so long, Lucy thought the Klamath County FSA camp was as close to heaven as a body could get on earth. She arranged all their things inside their tent just so. Pop's suitcase, turned on end, served as a table, and she topped it with one of Mama's doilies she'd carried all the way from Goodwell in her pasteboard box. When a family on

157

the other side of the camp moved on and left behind a length of calico, Lucy fetched it and stitched it to the back wall of the tent so they had something pleasant in view before they went to sleep. Widow Murphy next door loaned her a broom so she could sweep the floor each day. And she always made sure there was a biscuit left over from supper the night before for Pop's breakfast.

The first thing she put on each morning was a smile, hoping it would pass on to Pop the way a yawn did.

Sometime in the second week, when Pop started out the door to earn that week's rent, he noticed Lucy writing on her tablet.

"What's that scratching?" he asked in a voice that didn't sound like him, not one bit. It was the voice of someone so full of misery he might crack to pieces like a broken pitcher.

Lucy looked down at her lap and didn't answer for a minute. She measured out whether to tell the truth or not. Truth won out. "I was remembering that sampler Mama stitched that time. The one that said 'Count Your Blessings and They'll Double Up.'" She chewed on the end of her pencil. "So that's what I was doing. Counting my blessings."

With a sound of disgust, Pop snatched the tablet from her hand. "That's foolishness. Pure foolishness." He held her pad above his head. "I should throw this in the fire. Right this minute."

Lucy didn't say a word, but a pain went through her worse than anything she'd felt when Mama passed. It was one thing to lose a parent to death, but to lose a parent that was still living . . . Words hadn't been invented yet for that sort of sorrow.

"Oh, hang it all." Lucy ducked as Pop threw the tablet back at her. "I'll be late to work." He stomped off the platform onto the dirt path and headed to the camp manager's office. Lucy held the tent flap back, watching him go.

Widow Murphy was watching her.

"Do you need your broom back?" Lucy asked. "Let me get it for you." She ducked back inside to compose herself, then reemerged with the broom in hand. She hopped down from the platform and walked over to the widow's tent.

"It's best to let those kettles boil," Widow Murphy said, nodding her head after Pop. "He'll come around again. You'll see. This life is enough to sour up any man, even a good one like your daddy there."

Lucy nodded, her eyes welling with tears at the widow's kindness. She swiped them away quickly so no one could call her a crybaby.

Merrill FSA Camp, Klamath County, Oregon
April 18, 1940

Dear Gloria Jean,

You know how your mama says good things come in threes? Well, two good things happened today and I'm sure that means the third is on its way! This morning as I walked to the bathrooms, there next to the shower tent was a flash of yellow. You'll never

159

guess—it was a jonquil fighting like mad to meet the spring sun. I nearly picked it but decided to let it be so other folks could see its sunny face. Then, at the breakfast tent, there was even better news. The school district is going to send a bus so we camp kids can go to school! Some of the dumb oxes around here say they aren't going because it's so late in the school year. But better late than never is what I say!

I hope I'm not too far behind in my schooling. If only you were here to help me with arithmetic!

Friends forever,
Lucy

P.S. Widow Murphy pays me a nickel for fetching her water every day. I give most of it to Pop, but he lets me keep a penny a week. Though it's hard to resist the licorice whips at the camp store, I use my saved-up pennies to buy stamps so I can write you!

• • •

April 20, 1940
Goodwell, Oklahoma
Dear Lucy,

I sure hope that third good thing is that we get to come west soon. It is lonesome here in Goodwell without you. Your letters make you feel close, even though I know how far away we are from each other. Wearing your ribbon helps, too.

You will do just fine in school. You won't need my help with arithmetic as long as you remember *to read the whole story problem before you start to solve it.*

Daddy got a lead on a job in Texas. He's gone there for a spell. Me and Mama are working on setting a world's record for the number of ways to cook pinto beans.

When this Depression is over, I will never eat another bean in my entire life.

Friends forever,
Gloria Jean

The early May morning that Lucy started school put her to mind of starting school each year back in Goodwell. Mama would order her a new pair of saddle shoes from the Monkey Ward catalog. Pop would give her an apple to take to the teacher on the first day. And he always told her, "You get yourself an education. That's the ticket." But when she braided her hair that morning, he frowned. "We'd be out of this camp a whole sight faster if you kept working." Lucy's hands froze in place as she was twining the strands of her hair. She was afraid to remind him of his long-ago words. Afraid of him. She had never been afraid of her father before.

Ida Wolf called from outside the tent. "You ready to go, Lucy?"

Lucy didn't move.

"What are you standing there for?" Pop said. "I'll never hear the end of it from Widow Murphy if you don't go."

Lucy didn't wait a second longer. One braid unfinished,

she clomped across the floor in her pair of too-small boys' boots from the Charity Closet, slipping through the tent flap to meet Ida.

When the camp kids arrived at the big red-brick school building in town, this one kid in her class, Delbert White, heard Lucy's accent and started calling her "Licey" instead of Lucy. "Them Okies is covered with lice," he told his pals loudly. "They don't wash but once a year." Back home or in camp, Lucy wouldn't have thought twice about clocking him a good one. A shiner or a bloody nose might teach him a lesson. But here at school, she wanted to start off on the right foot. And fighting would not be a good way to make a first impression.

Especially not on Miss Olson, who was the daintiest thing Lucy had ever seen. She was soft-spoken, too. You had to crank your ears real hard to hear her. But lady that she was, she didn't hesitate to use the cane leaning up in the front corner of the room. Or so the other kids said. Leastways, everyone toed the line in Miss Olson's class.

Sometime near the end of the second week Lucy had been in school, Miss Olson stood at the front of the class with a look on her face that was practically rapturous. "I am delighted to tell you that my former college professor, Dr. Evans, is opening a new museum in town."

"I seen him," Missy Salters hollered out, without waiting to be called on.

Miss Olson raised one eyebrow. Her left.

"Sorry, ma'am." Missy raised her hand.

"Yes, Missy?"

"I seen him. At the old house where Mr. and Mrs. Ketteman used to live."

"That's correct. The Kettemans left their home to the university, with the request that it be used as a museum." She smiled again at her students. "And our class will have the opportunity to be among the first visitors. This coming Saturday."

Delbert hissed through his teeth. "I ain't giving up a Saturday for no museum," he said, loud enough for the students around him to hear.

Again Miss Olson's left eyebrow arched. Delbert's arm lumbered into the air like an injured goose. "I can't be excused from my chores on a Saturday," he said.

Miss Olson nodded. "I appreciate that that may be the case for some of you." Her eyes traveled around the room. "But those who can, please meet here at the school at ten a.m."

There was a question Lucy wanted to ask, but she would die before asking it. She sat there, chewing her pencil, when Miss Olson spoke out the answer. As if she'd read Lucy's mind.

"And the best part is that the Kettemans have left an endowment so that there is no admission fee. Ever!" She smiled warmly.

News traveled fast in the camp, and by suppertime, folks were talking about the museum visit. Lucy ate only half her biscuit, offering the other half to Pop. He'd never been a talker, and he'd been saying less and less the longer they'd been gone from Oklahoma. But there'd been a little bacon to throw in with the beans tonight and he seemed content as he reached for his pipe and tobacco after slurping up the last spoonful of supper.

"I hear that schoolteacher's up to something," he said, tamping the tobacco down in the bowl of his pipe.

Lucy nodded cautiously. "There's an excursion on Saturday. To the new museum." It wasn't exactly a question, but she held her breath anyway for his reply.

His pipe lit, Pop took a trial puff. "She needs to stick to the three Rs."

Though she wanted to beg and say, Please, let me go, Lucy held her tongue.

Pop stood up off his orange crate chair and it toppled over. "Going to go speak with the camp manager about a mill job. You get the supper things cleaned up and get ready for bed."

"Yes, sir." Lucy picked up Pop's plate.

He took a few steps away from the tent and then stopped. "You might as well go on Saturday. But see to it you're back in time to fix supper." He slapped at the tent flap as he went out, having gotten tangled in it. "I never thought I'd live someplace without a proper door." Anger greased his words.

Lucy stood for a moment, then called out to his retreating back, "Thank you, Pop."

That left the problem of what to wear. A person couldn't go to a fancy house turned into a museum wearing overalls and clodhopper boots. Boys' clodhopper boots, at that. She could let out the hem—again—in her cotton dress, but her feet were a problem. Seemed like she could just look at them and watch them grow. For the first day of school, she'd forced her feet into her old Mary Janes, but there was too much foot and not near enough shoe. She'd tried to make a trade for some shoes that fit, but nobody in camp had anything but broken-down oxfords or sneakers that were more hole than canvas.

She sat on an apple crate outside the tent, re-hemming her dress. Then, like a princess in one of those fairy stories Gloria Jean loved to read, Lucy discovered she, too, had a fairy godmother. Widow Murphy stepped out of her tent, holding something behind her back.

"These'll suit that dress better than those boots of yours." The old lady handed her a bundle wrapped up in an apron.

Lucy took the bundle and pulled away the fabric to reveal a pair of white t-strap shoes with a delicate kitten heel. "These are beautiful!"

Widow Murphy covered her mouth with her hand to hide her gap-toothed smile. "Them's what I wore on my wedding day." She held up her foot, ensconced in a man's work boot. "You'd never know it now, but I had real ladylike feet. Was one of my best features, Mr. Murphy always said."

"Oh, I can't borrow your wedding shoes." Lucy slowly held them back out to Widow Murphy, but not before noticing how close they appeared to be to her own size.

"You shore can," said the widow. "I'd be pleased as

165

punch to think they got an outing." She pushed the shoes back at Lucy. "Course, it'll cost you—"

Lucy's heart sank. She didn't have a cent and she couldn't ask Pop for anything.

Widow Murphy nodded solemnly. "Yep, I'll expect a good long visit afterward to hear about everything you seen."

Lucy let out the breath she'd been holding. "Yes. Oh, yes!" She wrapped the shoes back up in the apron, not even allowing herself to try them on. She would wear them only on museum day, that was all, to keep them as nice as she could.

Come Saturday morning, Lucy was the only camp kid up and dressed to hitch a ride into town with the iceman. If Miss Olson was disappointed to see that Lucy was by herself, she didn't let on. Waiting at the school were a tangle of town kids. Delbert White was not one of them, for which Lucy was thankful.

"Come, children," Miss Olson said to her baker's dozen of an entourage. Lucy, in Widow Murphy's wedding shoes, which turned out to be two sizes too big, wobbled up the walk in front of the Ketteman home. She was so struck by the outside of the house—with geegaws and curlicues and a little turret at the top that made her certain it was modeled after Rapunzel's castle—that she walked right out of the shoes without even noticing. Miss Olson's voice reminding them to mind their manners once inside snatched Lucy's thoughts back to the present. She quickly stepped back into the shoes and followed her teacher up the grand entry stairs.

Miss Olson's old professor, Dr. Evans, loved to hear himself talk. He yammered about this something-or-other and that doohickey in "this grand home" until Lucy's eyes were nearly spinning around in their sockets. After two eternities, he said that he was sure students of Miss Olson's would know how to conduct themselves in a place of history and that they were free to explore on their own, "without touching ANYTHING." Then he asked Miss Olson if she'd like to come to his office for tea, all the while stroking that caterpillar moustache on top of his lip.

All of the town kids buddied up, leaving Lucy the odd girl out, which suited her fine. That way she could wander at her own pace among the fascinations that filled every nook and cranny of the old mansion. At one point, Lucy found herself behind Betty Mitchell and Helen Frank; they turned right when they reached a T in the hallway, so she turned left, finding herself in a cozy little room labeled "The Land of the Sun." As she nosed around, she learned that the Land of the Sun was Japan. In a couple of the tramp camps they'd been in, Lucy had heard people bad-mouth the Japanese. "Trying to take all the jobs, the yellow devils," one man had said. Maybe that was why this room was tucked away in a far corner of the museum. But Lucy liked the things she saw in here—like that delicate teapot and those tiny cups without handles.

Paintings of mountains and seas captured with brushes as slight as a blade of grass somehow conveyed the power of those natural wonders. It was hard to attend to Dr. Evans' admonition not to touch when she came upon a tiny forest in a dish. "Bone-say-ee," she said aloud, trying to pronounce the name of this green delight. Imagine a real tree, hundreds of years old, no bigger than a cracker tin.

She was so engrossed in the bonsai that she exclaimed aloud when she encountered a pair of dark eyes. "Jumping Jehoshaphat!" she hollered, quickly clamping her hand over her mouth. "Sorry for being so loud, ma'am." Then she giggled at the realization that she was apologizing to a doll. Not a rag doll like Mama had made for her when she was a knee baby but a fancy thing. Fancier than any doll she'd ever seen in the Monkey Ward catalog.

She stepped closer and read the placard by the doll's display. "Miss Kanagawa. One of 58 Doll Ambassadors sent to the United States from the Schoolchildren of Japan." "Ambassadors," Lucy said aloud. "I don't know what that means, but it must be something important. You look like you were made to do something important." She reached her hand out to touch the doll's, but remembered Dr. Evans' words and pulled back.

❋

Ah, there is that tug again at my heart. Is this thin waif the one whose hand is on the other end of the kite string? The child for whom I was brought to this place?

She could certainly stand to eat a few bowls of donburi,

with some chicken cooked with the rice. Why do these Americans not feed their children properly? It must be another odd custom.

Like the custom of wearing a dress that is too small and shoes that are too large. It's certainly not very becoming.

✻

The hair on the back of Lucy's neck pricked up, as if she were being watched. For some reason, she suddenly felt the need to defend her footwear. "These are Widow Murphy's wedding shoes," she said aloud. "She loaned them to me. Trusted them to me." She glanced around and then giggled nervously. Here she was, talking out loud, when there was no one else in the room.

✻

Poor child. She mistakenly believes she is alone in this room. She does not yet know me.

But she will.

✻

On the wall behind the doll display was a map with a red pin to mark where the doll came from and a white pin to mark Klamath Falls. She had come a long way. "Was it hard to leave your home?" Lucy asked. "I miss Goodwell." She thought about these words for a moment. "I guess I don't exactly miss Goodwell. I miss Gloria Jean and Mama. And I miss having a house of our own. But Pop's working on that. I wish I could be more help."

169

***

Though this girl wears a cloak of sorrow, she has not let it weigh her down completely, like the old woman after Willie Mae's death.

I sense that her short life has been long on troubles. One parent gone and another who has lost his way, lost himself. And I see that a roof might be the beginning of the end to those troubles. Of course, I can only make suggestions. It is up to the child to take action.

And I am confident that she will. She is like me in that way. Samurai strong.

***

Once during a powerful dust storm—Mama was still alive then—Lucy had been out in the barn, playing with the new kittens. The rule was to get to the house as soon as the dust began blowing, so Lucy nestled the kitties back under their mother and ran to the house. The storm had kicked up a devil-dervish of static electricity, so that when Lucy touched the doorknob, she was knocked flat on her hind end from the shock. It was such a surprise, it didn't even hurt. Just like the jolt she got now, looking at that doll from Japan.

Hesitantly, she moved closer, examining the doll from the top of her silky black hair to the hem of her fancy dress. Behind her stood a trunk—a card said it was the trunk she and her belongings traveled in. "Some of her *accoutrement* are too delicate to be on display," the card said. Lucy would have to ask Miss Olson what *"accoutrement"* meant. Next to the doll a tiered stand displayed some of her belongings: a small silk purse, two paper fans, an ornately painted parasol. In front of the parasol was a miniature stationery set, complete with paper and envelopes.

"You write letters?" Lucy asked. "That's what I like to do, too. Gloria Jean says I write real interesting ones." At that moment, an idea popped into Lucy's mind. An idea she'd never have gotten if she hadn't wandered into this funny little room, tucked away in this big house.

Sharp laughter poked at her like a pencil point. "Look at that Okie." Lucy didn't need to turn around to know that Betty and Helen were behind her. "She's even dumber than I thought," said Betty. "Talking to a doll."

Lucy's eyes met Miss Kanagawa's and she felt another surge of energy. Not a jolt like the first time. But something that starched up her spine and unbent her shoulders. She walked past Betty and Helen with a firm smile and without a word, giving them no purchase for a squabble.

After she got home, she returned Widow Murphy's shoes and told her all about the museum.

"Why, I feel as if I was right there, taking it all in with you," the widow said after Lucy's report.

That gave Lucy the confidence to tell about her idea.

"I knew you was going to go places," said Widow Murphy when Lucy had finished. "That's just the ticket, seeing as most folks here can't neither read nor write." She fished out a penny. "I want to be your first customer."

Lucy ran home for her tablet and hurried back. Right then and there, she wrote out a letter to the widow's folks back home.

Word traveled fast. Soon Lucy had all the customers she could handle and then some. She found an empty Bright and Early coffee can and stashed away every cent she earned. She would never take any money to read mail, only to write letters in reply. By the time her birthday rolled around in July, that coffee can had a real musical jingle to it. Pop gave her a dime—one penny for each year she'd been alive—to spend any way she wanted, but she put that in the coffee can, too.

Merrill FSA Camp, Klamath County, Oregon
September 12, 1940

Dear Gloria Jean,

I'm sorry it has been so long since I've written. If your pop's still thinking of coming west, tell him Oregon's the place, not California. At first, Pop couldn't find any work but for helping around the camp. Then the camp manager took a liking to him— said he never saw Pop resting on a broom handle like some of the others—and got him a job at the railroad station, loading lumber. The sawmill manager, Mr. Hammond, took note of how hard Pop was working and came over to chew the fat. Pop said none of the folks he met in California ever took the time to do that. One thing led to another and Mr. Hammond found out that Pop knew a few

*things about wiring. So guess what! He's got a real,
honest-to-goodness job! He's an electrician at Mr.
Hammond's mill and his job is mighty important.
Mr. Hammond said he'd just as well burn dollar
bills if his machines weren't running. So that's what
Pop does: he keeps the machines running. The best
news of all is that Pop has his eye on a little house in
town. We've scribbled and tallied and figured out a
way to buy it. I'm helping, too, by writing letters for
folks at a penny a page. Long as old Betsy keeps
running and we stay healthy, we should be able to
swing it. And guess what?! It has two bedrooms, so
there is plenty of room for your whole family when
you come.*

Friends Forever,
Lucy

• • •

What with all the reading and writing she'd done over the
summer, and with a little tutoring from Miss Olson, Lucy
moved into the fifth grade come fall, along with the rest
of her class. Except for Delbert White. He got held back.

318 Oak Avenue
Klamath Falls, Oregon
May 12, 1941

Dear Mrs. Roosevelt,
*This is your friend Lucy Turner again. My new
teacher, Miss Ward, said you received over 110,000*

*letters last year. (My old teacher, Miss Olson, had to
quit teaching when she married Dr. Evans last
Christmas.) I never knew so many people like me
were writing to you. No wonder you couldn't write
back.*

*It's okay, though. I don't mind. You have plenty
on your plate, that is for sure! But I wanted to let you
know that Pop and me are doing fine. I'm in fifth
grade and get good marks in almost everything (Miss
Ward says I need to apply myself more to arithmetic).
I went to my first birthday party ever yesterday, for
Helen Frank. She has turned out to be a good friend,
though we started out on the wrong foot. Have you
noticed that sometimes people think because you don't
dress nice or talk the way they do, you can't be
friends? Helen said she is sorry she made that mistake
but it is all hunky-dory now between us.*

*Did you take note of the address at the top of this
letter? Pop and I have a house! Isn't that something,
us Okies living on Oak Avenue? You should see the
spring in Pop's step as he leaves for work each
morning. Anyway, we are doing just fine. Better than
fine, because Pop got Gloria Jean's father a job at the
mill, too. They aim to be here the end of next month.*

*So that's it. I figured you could use some good
news, so I wanted to let you know that Samuel and
Lucy Turner are okie-dokie.*

*Your friend,
Lucy Turner*

· · ·

Showing Gloria Jean all around Klamath Falls kept Lucy busy through the summer. On her birthday, July 12, she and Gloria Jean went to a double feature at the Star Theater in nearby Bly. Pop brought them home and they ate ham sandwiches with grape Nehi sodas for lunch— they each got their own bottle. Gloria Jean's mother had baked a birthday cake they were all going to share after supper that night. The girls were sitting on the front steps of 318 Oak Avenue sipping on their sodas when the mailman stopped. "Pretty fancy return address," he said, handing Lucy a letter.

June 27, 1941

Dear Miss Turner,

I do indeed need a dose of good news these days, especially with troubles brewing overseas. I am so delighted to learn of your good turn of fortune; I've never visited Klamath Falls but understand it is a lovely place.

You and your father are shining examples of my belief that what one has to do can usually be done.

With warm regards,
Eleanor Roosevelt

After reading it with Gloria Jean, Lucy showed the letter to Pop and Miss Olson—rather, Mrs. Evans—but no one else. It was so special that she didn't want to tarnish it by waving it around like one of those jokes on a bubble gum wrapper. The letter went into Mama's Bible for safekeeping, but Lucy brought it out every now and again when she needed comfort or encouragement.

Lucy never missed a Saturday at the museum, sometimes going with Gloria Jean but most often by herself. She found a good listener in Miss Kanagawa; she was able to talk to her about anything, even things she couldn't tell Gloria Jean. Like that one August day when she'd been thinking about Mama.

"Aunt Miriam says that it gets easier the more time that goes by. But it's been two years. And I still miss Mama. Still wish she was here," she'd told Miss Kanagawa. "Do you ever feel like that about folks?" She looked into those deep almond eyes. "I suppose dolls don't, really." Lucy shrugged her shoulders. "I'd miss *you*, if you went away," she said.

❋

I recall a time, in my early years, when I would not have been able to understand what Lucy was talking about. But I am older now, wiser. I know about the empty spaces left when dear ones leave our lives. My heart may be doll-sized, but when it comes to feeling, it is larger than a giant's.

❋

When Lucy noticed that Miss Kanagawa's dress—she learned it was called a kimono—was getting dingy, she and Pop made a wood and glass case, which they presented to the museum. As a gift. Dr. Evans was so pleased, he hired Pop to make some more display cases. There was soon so much work, in fact, that Pop asked Gloria Jean's father to help, and before they knew it they had a side business going. Lucy still longed to see the ocean, so Pop got it in his head to get a house for her there one day. "I may be an old man before it happens," he'd tell her as he looked over his bank statement, "but it's going to happen. I promise you."

One early December day when the town was decked out in green and red and gold for Christmas, something unspeakable happened. The Japanese navy bombed Pearl Harbor. Lucy and Gloria Jean held each other close as they sat transfixed in front of the radio, listening to the news.

❋

A few days ago, Dr. Evans stood before my display case, holding a newspaper in his trembling hand. Tears fell from his eyes like wet cherry tree blossoms. I couldn't imagine what had saddened him so.

He has now returned, at the back of a clump of men in felt fedoras and thin ties tight against their white-collared necks. I determined that they were members of the museum board.

"It's unpatriotic," one man said, his lips as thin as his dark tie. The other hats bobbed in agreement. "Everything in this room's got to go."

"Everything?" Dr. Evans asked.

The man with the thin lips frowned. "You could stash it all out of sight for a while. But it's probably best to get rid of it. Either way, we expect our decision to be carried out pronto."

When the men had gone, Dr. Evans walked from item to item in the Land of the Sun room. Then he stood in front of my case, head bowed, for a long time. I tried to let him know I understood. That I thought all would be well, someday. I do not know if my message was received.

He lifted me from the display case, gently set me inside my steamer trunk, and patted my cheek as if I were an anxious child. He said nothing, but I knew he meant to keep me safe. He quickly closed the lid of the trunk, and my world grew very quiet, very still.

I did not let myself think about Lucy. There are some things even a doll's small heart cannot bear.

※

Endings

If you want a happy ending, that depends, of course, on where you stop your story.

—ORSON WELLES

Mason Medcalf

Mason knew every board in the dock that led to Seal's place. And he usually ran all the way. Today, he walked, slowly, looking at but not really seeing the two rows of houseboats bobbing in the damp spring mist on either side of the wooden pier. Six on this side, five on the other. All of them looked pretty much the same, like day-old vanilla sheet cake with the frosting slumping off, except for the one on the far end, owned by a retired actor who'd fixed it up to look like a real house. A fancy house. It stood out like a peacock in a flock of chickadees.

He caught up with Mom in front of the fourth house-boat on the left. A yellow kayak hung like a happy-face smile from hooks under the eaves. A lace-leaf maple tree in a big wooden container stretched out its limbs next to the kayak.

"How is she now?" he asked. Seal wasn't sick, exactly. At least not with anything the doctors could fix with pills. Mom had explained it was Alzheimer's. Whatever it was, it creeped Mason out. He wanted his old Seal back. He didn't like this new one, this confused one. The last time he'd come, she hadn't even known who he was. That was why he hadn't been to visit in a long, long time. And he wouldn't have come today, either, except Mom threatened to confiscate his game player, permanently, if he didn't.

Mom shifted the basket she was carrying to her other arm. The aroma of cinnamon and apples tickled Mason's nose.

"Honestly, honey, I don't know. It's kind of a day-to-day thing." She gave Mason a wistful smile. "She knew me the other day. And Gloria Jean said she knew her, too, when she came to visit last week."

Mason's cousin, Emma, stood on the other side of Mom. Usually you couldn't find her "off" button, but today she was as quiet as a broken TV.

"Chin up, everybody." Mom stepped across the sliver of water separating the dock from the houseboat's front porch. "Oh, shoot. The key." She handed Mason the basket, heavy with Seal's favorite chicken and rice casserole and apple crisp, and fished in her pocket. "Don't tell me I left it at home."

"Can't the nurse let us in?" asked Emma.

"Oh, I hate to bother her. In case she's busy with Seal."

While Mom rummaged in another pocket, Mason stepped across to the porch. He lifted a stone from the planter with the tree in it and retrieved Seal's spare key.

"Brilliant!" Mom moved aside to allow him to unlock the door.

One of the things Mason always loved about Seal's house was its smell—a heady concoction of garlic, lemons, dust, and lake water. Now, he felt like he was going into a stranger's home. There wasn't even a hint of garlic. Mostly what he smelled was sour and mediciney.

He held the door for Mom and Emma. "Such a gentleman," Mom said. Mason ducked his head. He was no gentleman. He was trying to postpone going inside as long as he could.

"Hello? Abby? Seal?" Mom called. "It's Diane! And you'll never guess who's with me." She turned and made a face at Mason. "Say something," she mouthed.

He cleared his throat. "Seal?" He took a few steps toward her bedroom, which was opposite the cozy galley kitchen where he'd probably eaten a million pieces of French toast and a thousand bowls of split pea soup. "It's me. Mason." He couldn't move any closer. It was like a force field was keeping him back.

Abby, the nurse, stepped into the hall. Her face lit up when she saw them. "Oh, you kids will be just the ticket. She needs a bit of a lift today." She waved Mason and Emma into Seal's bedroom.

Somehow Mason stepped through the doorway. There was Seal—the person who'd taught him to ski and kayak

183

and who'd come to all his soccer games—lying as still as a doll in her four-poster bed. Her gray hair looked like some kind of gray moss growing all over the pillowcase. She was on her back, mouth open, breathing hard. What was that awful rattling sound?

Mom nudged him.

He stepped closer. Took a deep breath. "Seal?" he said again.

Seal opened her eyes. Looked right at him. "Delbert?" she asked. "What are you doing here? If you call me Licey one more time, I'll punch you. I swear."

Mason stepped back, looked at Mom. "It's me. It's Mason." He had no idea who Delbert was. Who Licey was. "Mason," he repeated.

Emma had followed him into the room. "Auntie Seal? This is Emma." She pointed to herself, then went to the far side of the bed and took one of Seal's knotty hands in hers. "We brought you some supper."

Seal turned her head. "Are there biscuits? Pop likes biscuits."

Mom called from the doorway. "Biscuits. And chicken. And dessert. How about that? Better than the Ritz." She laughed, but it was a fake laugh, pushed out through a tight throat.

"Biscuits," Seal repeated. Then she turned to Mason. "And not one for you, Delbert." She laughed a scary, witchy laugh.

Mason bolted and headed for the ship's ladder. Headed up to his room. Well, not his truly, but his whenever he came to stay. He grabbed the ladder's rails and began to climb. He burst through the opening at the top, launching himself into the familiar bedroom, the one he used to think was built for a Munchkin. Small and square, it held the basics: dresser, bed, desk. But the dresser's legs were cut off so it would fit under the angled ceiling. The "bed" was a mattress resting right on the floor. And the desk was an old door bracketed to the wall under a row of small-paned windows.

He walked over to the windows, dropped to his knees, and leaned over the desk to press his forehead against one small pane. His racing pulse began to slow. He took a few deep breaths. From here, he could see the Space Needle. When he was little, he used to pretend it was a spaceship that would take him back to his home planet. He'd been such a doofus. He turned his head so he could see the seaplanes land down at the other end of Lake Union.

He heard sniffling behind him.

Emma had followed him up the ship's ladder. She was sitting cross-legged on the mattress. Her nose was shiny and her eyes red. "I want Seal," she said, grabbing a pillow and hugging it close to her chest.

Mason was embarrassed by her dramatics, but he felt the same way. "I didn't think she would be this bad," he said.

Emma wiped her nose on the pillowcase. Then she began to cry in earnest.

He felt his own throat tighten. If this kept up, he'd be bawling himself.

"Hey, do you want to go in the attic?" That had always

185

been against the rules. Seal had been afraid one of them would put a foot between the joists, or something. But Seal wasn't in any condition to tell them to stay out and Mom was too busy with Seal to check on them.

"Sure." Emma ran her nose across the pillowcase one more time. "Let's go."

Whenever adults tell you to stay away from something, that something gains a powerful draw. Mason knew where the attic hatch was—had gotten close to opening it many times. He scooted across the floor to the far wall. "It's this door." He'd been about five when he discovered the hidden attic entrance, almost invisible in the bedroom wall.

The door was stiff. He put his shoulder into it. After three tries, it opened and he fell through.

"Shh!" Emma flapped her hands at him. "Your mom will hear."

"That was an accident." He shook himself and then wriggled through the now-open door. Emma followed. They balanced their way over to a section where some floorboards had been laid down. Mason was relieved to reach the secure surface. All those years of Seal telling him he could fall through the joists were hard to let go of.

"It's kind of creepy," said Emma, feeling her way to the safe spot next to Mason. "Do you think there are spiders?"

"Only poisonous ones."

Emma squeaked. "What?" She began scrambling toward the door.

Mason grabbed her foot. "Just kidding."

"That was mean!" But Emma said it with a laugh.

They sat quietly for a few minutes, looking over the jumble of boxes and trunks and stuff. "Remember when Seal let us eat strawberry shortcake for breakfast, lunch, and dinner that time?" Emma hugged her knees to her chest. "And how she always made a treasure hunt for us to find our birthday presents?"

Remembering those things made Mason feel worse, not better. He got on his hands and knees and began exploring. "Hey, look at this." He held up an old record.

Emma read the label. "It says 'Hawaiian Love Song.' I wonder what they played these on."

"A record player, dummy." Mason flipped open the lid of a nearby cardboard box. "Hey, here are Seal's Christmas decorations." He gently pulled out a blown-egg ornament, made before his mom was even born, decorated with red felt and cotton to look like a Santa head.

"Careful with that," Emma said. She tugged at an old suitcase, trying to open it. "Do you know how to pick locks?"

Mason made a face. "We haven't gotten to that unit in school yet." He scootched past Emma to the very back corner of the attic. Under a moth-eaten army blanket he found a trunk. And it wasn't locked. He pushed the levers and they clicked open. He lifted the lid.

A pair of eyes stared back at him.

"*Aaah!*" He fell back.

Oh, to feel a bit of light again. It's lovely. Lovely. If I could move my limbs, I would indulge in a glorious stretch. But for now I will be content to be out of the darkness.

It appears that a boy is the one who opened my trunk. Strange creatures, boys. They tend to avoid dolls and thus avoid me. I recall Brigitte telling me they were smelly, with disgusting things in their pockets. This one doesn't look so bad. And I don't smell anything but dust.

❋

"What is it? A rat?" Emma squirmed her way to Mason and peeked over his shoulder. "You yelled about a doll?"

"I was surprised, okay?"

Emma nudged him out of the way. "She looks Japanese. Where do you think Seal got her?" She set the doll on the floor and rummaged in the trunk. "Look at all this stuff in here." She pulled out a small teapot and a torn silk parasol. "Some of this doesn't look like it belongs. A marble? And this handkerchief doesn't look Japanese." She shook it out. "Not with yellow airplanes on it."

A piece of paper fluttered to the floor when Emma lifted out the printed handkerchief. Mason picked it up. He couldn't read it very well—the writing was all faded. He could make out something about words and birds. He folded the paper up carefully and put it back in the trunk. "This stuff might be valuable. It looks pretty old."

*

There is a cloud over these children, especially the boy. I sense a loss, not unlike the one Lucy experienced when the hard times changed her father so.

Was I awakened by this boy's need? Is he the one I am to help? I have been asleep so long that my mind is as useful as one chopstick. Perhaps it is best to wait. To watch. To listen.

*

Mason didn't like the way Emma had set the doll face-down on the floor. He turned it over. "Hey," he said. "Let's take this downstairs. Ask Seal about it." He wasn't sure where the idea had come from, but now that he'd said it aloud, he liked it.

"I'll be down in a minute," said Emma. "I want to look around some more."

Mason gingerly picked up the doll. The last thing he wanted to do was break it getting it down the ship's ladder. But he managed safely.

"What have you got there?" Mom was coming out of Seal's bedroom carrying a teacup.

"Uh. We found it. In the attic," Mason answered.

Mom frowned. "You know that's off-limits." But she didn't sound too mad. "It's pretty. I've never seen it before. I wonder if it was Seal's when she was a kid." Mom filled the teakettle and set it on the burner. "Were you going to show it to her?" She smiled at him. "That's a

189

great idea. Sometimes the past is an easier place for her to be."

The doll slid around a bit in Mason's arms. He felt goofy holding it. Good thing none of his friends could see him.

"Go on in. I'll be there in a minute. Abby went out to grab some lunch and Seal wanted another cup of tea." She lifted the tea tin down from the cupboard.

Mason took a deep breath and stepped into the bedroom, holding the doll out in front of him like a shield.

"Oh!" Seal struggled to sit up in bed when she saw what he carried. "Miss Kanagawa!" Her voice sounded younger. Almost girlish.

❋

It is a shock to see an old friend so gray and wrinkled. But I would recognize those eyes anywhere. All those hours we spent together, there in the museum. She would come to me, eyes damp with discouragement and pain, and by the time she left, they would be lit with hope.

❋

Seal laughed a Seal laugh. A real laugh. It made the knot in Mason's stomach loosen a bit. "My old friend," she said. "Oh, do we have stories to tell!" She took the doll from Mason and set it on one side of her in the bed. She patted the other side for Mason to come sit. He did. Mom slipped in with Seal's tea and perched on the chair at the vanity.

"I hope you never have to live through a time like that. The Dirty Thirties, some folks called it. We lost the farm, Mama . . ." Seal's eyes seemed to be focused on something far away from her bedroom in a houseboat on Lake Union in Seattle. "And lost our way, Pop and I." And she told them the story of how she and her father left Oklahoma for California. And how they ended up in some kind of camp in Oregon. It was a sad story. Mason saw Mom wipe her eyes every now and then.

"Then Dr. Evans opened the museum, and when I saw Miss Kanagawa"—Seal stroked the doll's black hair— "I knew I'd found a friend. When the war broke out, they didn't want her anymore. Didn't want anything Japanese. Dr. Evans bought her from the museum with his own money. And he gave her to me." She shook her head. "He and his wife, my old schoolteacher, were both so good to me."

"How did you end up in Seattle?" Mason asked.

"When Pop passed, he left me enough money that I could finally live by the water." She chuckled. "Never dreamed I'd live *on* it! That's something for a little old Okie gal."

Emma wandered in, holding a piece of paper, as Seal was telling about picking hops in Yakima for a penny a pound.

"Hey, Seal," Emma said, "is this letter really from Eleanor Roosevelt?" She brought it over to the bed.

Seal stroked the yellowed paper. "I must have written her a dozen letters. Never dreamed she'd answer me."

"That's you?" Emma asked. "Lucy?"

"For Lucille." Seal handed the letter back to her. "I outgrew Lucy, and then, when I met Clarence, he called me Seal."

Mom got up from her chair and went to stand by the bed. "I never knew that was how you got your nickname." She took Seal's hand in hers.

"I like this part," Emma said, pointing to the letter. "Where she says, 'What one has to do can usually be done.'"

Mom looked over Emma's shoulder. "We should get it framed. And put it over by the mirror so you'd see it every day."

Seal sighed. "That'd be real nice."

The afternoon felt like Christmas to Mason, with each one of Seal's stories—stories he'd never heard her tell before—like a gift that had been forgotten under the tree and newly discovered. He felt like he had his old Seal back. When he thought about it, it had started when he brought in that worn-out doll. It wasn't until she saw Miss Kanagawa that Seal really got to talking.

Mason shook his head at such a crazy thought. How could that old thing have made a difference? It was like Mom said. Seal was going to have good days. And bad days. They lucked out that today was one of her good ones.

Seal shifted in the bed, to face Mom. "Gloria Jean, you said you were going to help me with my arithmetic," she said. "You promised."

Mason and Emma exchanged glances. As quickly as she'd slipped out of her confusion, Seal had slipped back into it.

Mom pulled a tissue from her pocket and blew her nose quietly. "Well, I always keep my promises," she said. "But maybe you should get some rest first."

"I am feeling tuckered out. I guess I've a right to be. I picked thirty-two pounds of beans this morning." Seal settled back, head on the pillow, and tucked an arm around Miss Kanagawa.

Mason turned off the bedside lamp and tiptoed out of the room behind Mom and Emma. He turned back to look at Seal resting there, that doll in her arms. The dark must have been playing tricks on his eyes. It looked like there was a tear rolling down the doll's cheek.

Seal said something as he was about ready to step over the threshold. "What?" he asked.

"See you tomorrow?"

He thought about that line in the Eleanor Roosevelt letter. That what a person has to do can be done. He patted his hand on the door frame.

"I'll be here," he told her.

✳

I may be showing signs of age, like my friend Lucy—my kimono frayed, my joints stiff, and my gofun face cracking—but the nerve of that boy to think that because I am old and worn out I cannot help people!

193

I will be faithful to the task for which I was created until I am so far beyond repair that not even one such as Master Tatsuhiko could mend me.

Until then, there is a boy with a lesson to learn.

And no one better to teach him than I.

✳

AUTHOR'S NOTE

Bunny's Story

Belle Wyatt Roosevelt did indeed accept Miss Japan on behalf of the children of New York in a ceremony at City Hall, attended by Mayor Jimmy Walker. One story has it that the doll *did* wobble in her arms when the envoy handed it to her. The dolls really were on display at Lord & Taylor for ten days when Mr. Reyburn was the company president. Though *Town Topics* was a 1920s periodical, I created the news story "Little Envoys Arrive in Town," but I can't take credit for the delicious expression "Fifth Avenoodle," which I found in an issue of the magazine. I am also grateful to have discovered Eric Homberger's *The Historical Atlas of New York City: A Visual Celebration of 400 Years of New York City's History*, which helped me imagine the New York City that Bunny moved around in.

I am certain that the real Belle Wyatt Roosevelt, granddaughter of Theodore Roosevelt, twenty-sixth president of the United States, was a lovely child; however, since I invented Bunny, I also invented Belle's less-than-pleasant personality to add tension to the story.

Lois' Story

It's hard to imagine that the city of Chicago would dare host a World's Fair in 1933, smack-dab in the middle of the Great Depression, but it did. And the fair was such a hit it was extended into 1934. Thanks to an engaging website, www.cityclicker.net/chicfair, and a lovely book called *Chicago's 1933–34 World's Fair, A Century of Progress in Vintage Postcards*, by Samantha Gleisten, I was able to find out a great deal about the exhibits, the fairgrounds, and the Sky Ride. Neither Miss Kanagawa nor any of the other dolls I describe was actually displayed at the fair, but I reasoned that if the organizers allowed such novelties as the Mills Freak Show, alligator wrestling, and something called the Great Beyond, they would have readily welcomed an exhibit of dolls from around the world.

Willie Mae's Story

President Franklin D. Roosevelt's New Deal was a lot about creating New Jobs. In 1935, the Works Progress Administration, or WPA (renamed the Work Projects Administration in 1939, and sometimes called We Poke Along, by skeptics), was created to help put people to work. One of the jobs created was that of packhorse librarian, which you can read more about in Kathi Appelt and Jeanne Cannella Schmitzer's wonderful book *Down Cut Shin Creek: The Pack*

Horse Librarians of Kentucky. Willie Mae's brother worked for the Civilian Conservation Corps, or CCC, as did 250,000 other men, eighteen years old and older, helping to plant trees and build dams, fire towers, and park trails, in addition to many other public projects.

Lucy's Story

One of the many things I remember my beloved grandmother telling me was that she hoped I would never have to live through a depression, as she had in the "Dirty Thirties," when millions of people were out of work. During the Great Depression, people lost everything—their businesses, their homes, and, like Lucy's Pop, their pride and hope. While I grew up hearing my grandmother's stories about those hard times, I got a specific picture of the plight of the Okies from *Children of the Dust Bowl: The True Story of the School at Weedpatch Camp*, by Jerry Stanley. And giving truth to the saying that one picture is worth a thousand words, I found the photographs in *Daring to Look: Dorothea Lange's Photographs and Reports from the Field*, by Anne Whiston Spirn, and *The Depression Years: As Photographed by Arthur Rothstein* (published by Dover Press) invaluable.

Like Lucy, thousands of people, adults and children alike, wrote to Eleanor Roosevelt during the Great Depression. They asked for money, clothes, and even bicycles. Between 1933 and 1940, she received nearly seven hundred thousand letters. As often as she could, Mrs. Roosevelt wrote back. I'm sure she would have answered Lucy's letter had she seen it, but the reply in this book was written by me, not Mrs. Roosevelt.

The Friendship Dolls did indeed travel around this entire

country. According to Dr. Gulick's own report (*Dolls of Friendship: The Story of a Goodwill Project Between the Children of America and Japan*, Second Edition, Sidney L. Gulick), "Between January and July [1928] welcome receptions were given the dolls in every state but two of the Union. The towns and cities visited . . . numbered four hundred and seventy-nine." I found no record, however, that any Friendship Doll visited Klamath Falls, Oregon. That was another of my inventions for the sake of the story.

The Friendship Dolls

In November of 1927, fifty-eight Friendship Dolls arrived in the United States as a gift from Japanese schoolchildren. The dolls were about three feet tall, with black human hair—cut into a bob with bangs—and handpainted faces. Their pearl-white "skin" was not porcelain but *gofun*, a material made from crushed oyster shells. Each doll was dressed in an elegant silk kimono and was equipped with dozens of accessories, including lacquer chests, tea sets, parasols, and even a passport.

The dolls were feted and admired as they traveled around the country, eventually finding homes, primarily, in various museums. After the bombing of Pearl Harbor, on December 7, 1941, many of them were removed from display, sold, lost, perhaps even destroyed. Only one doll remained on exhibit during World War II. That was Miss Kagawa (not the Miss Kanagawa of this story), at the North Carolina State Museum. After the attack on Pearl Harbor, she was turned to face the wall, and a sign was placed next to her. It began: "Whom the Gods Would Destroy, They First Make Mad."

I learned about the Friendship Dolls when I was in

Montana, conducting research for *Hattie Big Sky*. In the basement of the Montana Historical Society Museum in Helena, I came across a photo of a blond farm girl in overalls standing next to a remarkable Japanese doll, nearly her size. They came from such different worlds—that hardscrabble girl and that elegant doll—I couldn't imagine how they got together. I had never heard of these dolls before, and when I returned home, I set to learning as much as I could about these diminutive ambassadors of peace and goodwill. I have seen two of the dolls: Miss Tokushima, who is housed in Spokane, Washington, at the Northwest Museum of Arts and Culture (thank you, Laura Thayer and Rose Krause), and Miss Shizuoka, in Kansas City, Missouri, at the Union Station Kansas City Museum (thank you, Lisa Shockley). I am not embarrassed to say that these dolls spoke to me, delivering a loud and clear message: Tell our story! I hope that through this book I can, in some small way, pass on their message of friendship and peace.

Since 1980, many people have worked to keep the spirit of the Friendship Dolls alive. Sidney L. "Denny" Gulick III, grandson of Dr. Sidney Gulick, the initiator of the doll exchange program, and his wife, Frances, continue the Friendship Doll tradition in their own way. Bill Gordon (http://wgordon.web.wesleyan.edu/dolls/japanese) maintains a complete and informative website that describes both the American blue-eyed baby dolls first sent to Japanese schoolchildren and the Torei Ningyo—"return gift dolls" or Friendship Dolls—sent to America in return. Many others, especially Michiko Takaoka, Rosie Skiles, and Rosalie Whyel, have worked tirelessly to educate others about these amazing dolls.

Though this story is based on actual historical events, this is a work of fiction. I have created news articles—for example, the one on page 43—and places—the museums in Lexington, Kentucky, and Klamath Falls, Oregon—to help make this story real.

One thing is completely true: to date, thirteen of the original fifty-eight dolls, including the Miss Kanagawa of this story, are still missing.

ACKNOWLEDGMENTS

Thank you to my first readers, Bonny Becker, Kathryn Galbraith, Sylvie Hossack, Dave Patneaude, and Mary Nethery; to my agent, Jill Grinberg; to Rebecca Short; and to all of the people who generously shared their knowledge and expertise as I researched this book. My biggest thanks are reserved for my editor, Michelle Poploff, a woman with the patience of Job.

ABOUT THE AUTHOR

Though she tried hard to keep her mind on track while researching her previous book, *Hattie Big Sky*, when Kirby Larson ran across a 1920s photo of a Montana farm girl in overalls standing next to an exquisite Japanese doll, she couldn't keep her imagination quiet. What brought the two together? Kirby did some initial research to satisfy that curiosity, but it would be five long years before she could turn her full attention to the Friendship Dolls' story.

A passionate writer of historical fiction, Kirby also collaborates with her dear friend Mary Nethery on nonfiction picture books, such as the award-winning *Two Bobbies: A True Story of Hurricane Katrina, Friendship, and Survival*.

Kirby Larson lives in Kenmore, Washington, with her husband, Neil, and Winston the Wonder Dog. You can visit her at kirbylarson.com.